To: Dear Mario
With M...
Bra...

FOUR MASKS
OF
DECEPTION

✳
you cousin Parole!

Bradley Bernarde

SCRIPTORA

Published in Great Britain 2021 by

SCRIPTORA
25 Summerhill Road
London N15 4HF
in association with SWWJ
(Society of Women Writers & Journalists)

www.swwj.co.uk

ISBN: 978-0-9500591-6-7

Printed and bound by Witley Press Hunstanton PE36 6AD
www. witleypress.co.uk

As someone who has enjoyed the many benefits of SWWJ membership for over thirty years I am dedicating this book to those of you I am privileged to call friends.

My most sincere thanks to Chief Executive Katie Childs and her staff for allowing me to use Chawton House as the fictional Hawton where events occur which would never have been allowed in Miss Austen's day!

My thanks also to SCRIPTORA and Mary Rensten for her valuable advice and guidance.

Cover design: GREENGilbert

After completing a creative writing course Bradley published a number of short stories in national magazines, but it was *The Apothecary's Gift*, set in Regency England and published by Whydown Books in 2003 (later republished as an e-book with the title *Twelve Days to Dream*) that launched her career as a novelist. She then travelled back to the seventeenth century and the Commonwealth with *To Thine Own Self*, to be followed by the vastly different e-book, *Pas de Deux for a Cop*, a twentieth century thriller set in New York. Awaiting publication is a family saga, *Yoke of Heaven,* based on her own family history, in which Jewish and Christian families prove that understanding one another can unite them in true affection.

Bradley is a member of the Society of Authors, a member of the Emile Zola Society, and a Fellow and Vice President of the Society of Women Writers & Journalists.

1

The ball bounced from step to step down the stairway, before landing on Sir Robert Masters' highly polished boot. He looked up askance.

'No!'

But it was too late; Edward's small head was already wedged between the banisters and he let out a frightened wail: 'I's stuck!' while his sister Lucy stared in fascination at what appeared to be her twin's guillotined torso.

Sir Robert leapt for the stairs, but before he was half way up his entire staff of twelve, having been alerted by Edward's cry, materialised from their quarters. Despite feeling helpless, Sir Robert continued to the landing. As he approached Edward's wails lessened to gulps, while Lucy announced complacently: 'He's still stuck.'

'So I see,' Sir Robert replied, annoyed that instead of sounding sarcastic he sounded worried instead.

Having created havoc, Edward stopped crying and settled comfortably into his difficult pose, while everyone began making suggestions as to extrication; then a voice boomed from the floor above and Symons, the butler, descended the stairs.

'Butter, Sir Robert, it requires butter.'

With his dignity and immense girth dwarfing all around him, Symons merely had to raise an eyebrow in the direction of the nearest footman, and the man departed hurriedly in search of the aforementioned butter.

Some time later, having despatched his greasy nephew to be washed by his nursemaid Hetty, the only female in an otherwise exclusively male establishment, Sir Robert sat in his library reflecting on just how his life had been disrupted since the twins' arrival four years earlier.

Stunned by the death of his brother Graham and sister-in-law Olivia in a carriage accident, Sir Robert had found a certain solace as the twins' only living relative, in accepting responsibility for their welfare and guardianship. He had seen it not only as his duty, but as an extension of his natural concern for vulnerable beings, and those less fortunate than himself.

A man of charm and refinement Sir Robert had, for the majority of his thirty-five years, participated in the established London season from habit, rather than desire. Occasionally he would even ignore fashionable convention and on the pretext of a headache, or some other minor disability, spend an evening in the tranquillity of his beloved library, with its many classical volumes packed tightly along shelves around the room.

Not that Sir Robert was unaware that the flamboyancy and wealth exhibited by his peers constituted a very small part of the country's true condition. The difficulties experienced by the less privileged during the present upheavals of the Regency years were something of which he had a personal knowledge. As an admirer of the late

Thomas Coram, he had visited the benefactor's refuge for homeless children and seen how, but for that institution, they might have been led into a life of crime and corruption.

Appalled by what he had learned at the Foundling Hospital, he had decided to witness for himself the areas from which these children had been rescued, and after days of wandering through the areas of Tothill Fields, Bermondsey and Bethnal Green, Sir Robert had become determined to try and rescue some of the waifs he encountered.

But he soon discovered that this was by no means as easy as he had anticipated. For, despite his enthusiasm, he had so far only succeeded in persuading four miscreants to relinquish their so-called apprentices. Aware that his friends would have considered him eccentric, if not deranged, Sir Robert had taken care that only Harold Sinclair, that most discreet of servants at his country estate, Hawton Hall in Hampshire, knew the true identities of Albert, Johnny, Patsy and Grace, the small boys and girls now being trained as pages and serving maids.

Despite this philanthropy, Sir Robert's true personality was not apparent in the rather reserved, self-confident image he exhibited to his contemporaries. From his earliest youth, possibly because he had been blessed with an affectionate and demonstrative family, he had sought out individuals who had been denied the advantages he enjoyed,. Even as a small boy, he had nurtured abandoned animals and later persuaded his parents to permit families who had been made homeless by one of the Enclosure Acts on other estates, to shelter in empty Hawton cottages.

Not that Sir Andrew and Lady Masters needed a great deal of persuasion; contrary to many of their contemporaries they were acutely aware of the differences existing between those of their own station and the less fortunate. The first twenty years of their married life had included the French Revolution, which exposed the appalling conditions suffered by France's plebeian classes when compared with the comforts enjoyed by the aristocracy and bourgeoisie.

As one of the very few educated Englishmen who realised the dangerous effects the horrors across the Channel could have on the less fortunate, it was one of Sir Andrew's great disappointments that the French experience seemed to have made no impression on those of his own countrymen in power, and he always regarded it as a valuable lesson never fully appreciated by his contemporaries.

However, he did not let the lesson go untaught in his own home; he spent many hours explaining to his sons that it was their responsibility to ensure that the under-privileged should be aided whenever possible, and it was this maxim which encouraged Sir Robert in his philanthropy.

Now contemplating his nephew's latest misdeed he smiled to himself, as he stretched his legs out towards the fire. Apart from being his retreat from society, the library also served as an escape from any uncertainties of the day, and since the twins' arrival they had not been infrequent.

Reflecting its owner's preference for simplicity the large room contained only three comfortable looking high-backed Louis XV chairs, a stepladder, and a Pembroke table. Because of the modicum of furniture, the pale blue curtains and paintwork could have appeared cool and unwelcoming but for the high-backed fire in the grate, Challenger the spaniel sleeping on the hearth, and the happy smile on the portrait of Sir Robert's mother, hanging above the mantle-shelf.

Glancing up at the painting he now gave it a rueful grin; despite the disruptions he knew she would have approved of his action, and comforted by this thought, he was about to pick up the book he had been reading when he heard the sound of running footsteps from somewhere outside the house, accompanied by a woman's scream.

Immediately Challenger awoke and began growling and Sir Robert gave him a reassuring pat, but before he could do anything further there was a tap on the door and his valet, Wenders, entered.

'Please forgive this second disturbance, Sir Robert, but it was from Millie, Rivers' daughter, returning home to the mews. As she approached the entry she believed she was about to be attacked.' Wenders' usually implacable expression was concerned. 'There was a commotion on the other side of the square, and it would appear that there has been yet another attack not far from here.'

Sir Robert frowned. Rivers Newsome was the Head Coachman, and Millie was known to be an unflustered girl so her present reaction was unusual.

'For such a calm girl to behave so, she must have been greatly disturbed,' he declared. 'And this is the third time there has been such a disruption within the last twelve days. Have not the Bow Street Foot Patrol been summoned? And the Watch, was he not to hand? And what of Millie, has she been harmed?'

'No, Sir Robert, merely scared and so far as I can ascertain, neither constabulary was in the vicinity. If you wish, Sir Robert, I can send a message for a Runner to attend.'

'No matter,' Sir Robert sighed. 'If Millie is safe all is well. I fear we live in a violent age, Wenders. I was but a few weeks old when Lord Gordon's petition unleashed the mob in London, and despite our many Governments' attempts since, it seems the criminal populace can still rampage at will even in streets such as ours. Is there aught else? You appear still concerned.'

'While I am present, Sir Robert,' Wenders hesitated to control a slight cough before continuing, 'I would be most grateful for a few moments of your time.' Wenders' coughs always preceded a problem and Sir Robert glanced warily at his valet.

'It is the young master and mistress, Sir Robert. Forgive the liberty of my suggesting such a thing, but have you ever considered a governess?'

It was the first time Wenders had ever referred to the twins, despite having lived with them for four years; and long ago Sir Robert had decided, that by persistently ignoring them Wenders had succeeded in convincing himself that they did not exist.

'A governess?' Sir Robert now repeated, somewhat bemused. 'Are they not a little too young?'

'Oh no, Sir Robert.' Wenders shook his head emphatically. 'I understand from my friend Mr. Beech, who is valet to Lord Hardington, that a governess has already been engaged for Lord Charles and he is a mere eight months.'

'Gracious,' Sir Robert exclaimed. 'But I very much appreciate your interest Wenders. I shall have to consider the matter.'

'Of course, Sir Robert.' Wenders gave his customary slight bow. 'It was just that if you did decide to proceed with such an arrangement, I am in a position to recommend such a personage. Although, Sir Robert, I intend in no way to be presumptuous,' he added quickly.

Sir Robert was intrigued. Unlike many of his contemporaries he had always taken a personal interest in the lower ranks amongst his servants, and was well acquainted with their pursuits; but he had refrained from intruding into the lives of his senior staff, considering their status entitled them to privacy. Which was why, despite Wenders having been recommended to Sir Robert by his late mother when both men were in their early twenties, he was ignorant of any associations or interests his valet might have outside the environs of Grosvenor Square. He now studied Wenders with considerable interest.

'How opportune that you should know such a person,' he replied. 'Has she extensive knowledge of very young children?'

'Indeed sir, she only recently left her last position in a church school where she instructed small children in all the academic subjects, and she is very well versed in French, a language of which she is most fond.'

'And how well is she known to you?' Sir Robert asked, even more intrigued.

'Very well, Sir Robert, she is my sister.'

Only his excellent breeding controlled Sir Robert's features.

'Thank you, Wenders,' he replied. 'I will give the matter some thought, and if I decide on adopting your suggestion perhaps your sister, Mrs, Miss?'

'Mrs. Amanda Brace, Sir Robert.'

'*Mrs.* Brace?' Sir Robert repeated questioningly. 'Forgive me for asking Wenders, but may I enquire as to her present marital status?'

'I very much regret she is a widow, Sir Robert. Her husband died some fourteen months ago, and as the union was childless and Mr. Brace did not leave any capital to speak of, my sister has been forced to seek employment in the only capacity available to her.'

Sir Robert nodded understandingly. 'Thank you, Wenders, and I will as I said, give the matter some thought before making a decision.'

As the door closed behind Wenders, Sir Robert contemplated their conversation with some apprehension, but he was also intrigued. When his mother had recommended Wenders so enthusiastically all those years ago she had, Sir Robert now recalled, mentioned that the applicant had a very young sister living with his mother. So in a way, Sir Robert reflected, the fact that Mama was aware of her existence could I suppose be regarded as a sort of testimonial, if a somewhat vague one.

But the idea of admitting another woman into his almost bachelor household still did not appeal. All house-keeping duties were supervised by Symons and his minions, and since his mother's death Sir Robert had always confined his entertaining to Hawton Hall; thus ensuring that no women crossed the threshold at Grosvenor Square, until Hetty arrived carrying the twins.

Any fashionable lady who was so adventurous as to climb the entrance steps in an attempt to leave her card was obliged to retreat, after being advised politely but firmly that Sir Robert was not at home.

The idea of a governess also reminded him of a brief episode during his own, otherwise happy childhood, when his parents had misguidedly employed a thin angular woman called Miss Finch to teach their two young sons the '3 Rs'.

Unfortunately the only knowledge imparted into her pupils during her two weeks employment, was fear. A circumstance discovered by Lady Masters when she heard Robert screaming in pain, as Miss Finch thrashed him for some trivial misdemeanour.

Although his persecutor was immediately dismissed and his anguish assuaged by his mother, the experience was responsible for Sir Robert's aversion to any form of corporal punishment. Even at Harrow he had somehow managed to avoid being birched, and he found most distressing, the idea of his charges being made to suffer his own painful experience.

Now, once again alone in the library, he sank into the nearest chair and tried to decide whether to pursue

Wenders' suggestion. Although the children had disrupted his life, the novelty of their presence had also helped ease the mental anguish he had experienced on realising that with the tragedy of their parents' deaths, all those who had known him and loved him best, no longer existed.

But apart from Sir Robert's tenderness towards the defenceless, it was also his natural love for the twins that was responsible for his regular visits to the nursery to indulge them excessively on each occasion.

As all the twins' needs were administered to by Hetty, who rarely left the nursery wing except to promenade her charges in the square, Sir Robert's life had not, for the first two years, been substantially affected. But the twins were now four years old, and Sir Robert was beginning to realise, albeit reluctantly, that their natural curiosity and especially Edward's mischievous ways, needed the ministrations of someone experienced in all aspects involved in the care of growing children. And in view of their extreme youth, and despite Sir Robert's reservations, he realised that *someone* would have to be a woman.

Having at last come to this inevitable verdict, he rang the bell for Wenders and explained his decision.

'Perhaps then you could kindly request Mrs. Brace to attend, so that we can discuss the matter. However,' Sir Robert added firmly, 'there is one point on which I insist. I wish her to know prior to our meeting that I will not, in any way, permit any form of thrashing to be administered to the children. No matter what kind of misbehaviour she may encounter.'

If Wenders was surprised by such a remark, his only response was his customary bow before he left the room.

Sir Robert watched the door close with some apprehension. It was not that he was averse to the female sex. He just did not relish the prospect of them interfering in any way in his life. Despite his late mother's attempts to interest him in eligible alliances, Sir Robert had contemplated marriage only once.

Having been raised by adoring parents who had, possibly unwisely, instilled into their sons the belief that anyone they loved would be as trusting and devoted as themselves, Sir Robert had assumed that his first object of real passion at twenty-four would have the same excellent qualities as his mother.

But the fact that the adored one, the daughter of a landowner in the same county, proved fickle, by promising to be his devoted wife while planning to elope with her father's coachman, had destroyed Sir Robert's belief in female probity.

Even his brother's very happy marriage as an example of what could be achieved had no effect, and Sir Robert had remained aloof from any further emotional entanglements. Apart from the occasional discreet dalliance with a lady of the town, he treated all his female acquaintances with infinite courtesy, and cool indifference.

Occasionally, he had felt that perhaps his life lacked the intimacy of a loving union, but the feeling rarely lasted long and was usually banished by his customary retreat into one of his much loved classics, or the works of Thomas Paine, or Arthur Young.

Yet despite his lack of enthusiasm for female company, Sir Robert was still a supporter of female education, an interest originally aroused by his mother. As a young woman, she had become acquainted with Elizabeth Montagu, and had been a regular visitor to her meetings where she had met men and women with similar views. She had also been an admirer of Mary Wollstoncraft, and introduced her son to that writer's book *A Vindication of the Rights Of Woman*, the views of which Sir Robert strongly endorsed.

Perhaps it was because he felt less vulnerable with a woman who attempted to interest his mind rather than his emotions, that his few female acquaintances were mainly middle-aged, and known for their intellect rather than their allure. For this reason, Sir Robert also sympathised with the beliefs of the reformer, Henry Hunt, who believed that the country's political system should be based on universal suffrage, and the ballot.

After all, Sir Robert reasoned to himself, if a woman can carry the next generation and care for it to adulthood, sometimes with very little assistance from others, she is entitled to the same privileges as the male population.

Aware his radical views would be considered scandalous by most of his acquaintances, Sir Robert had always kept his thoughts to himself since the death of his brother, but he sometimes longed for the chance to reveal his opinions to a sympathetic ear.

He glanced down towards the fire where Challenger was now sleeping contentedly, and tried to imagine Mrs. Brace's appearance. Would she be fat and squat, or tall angular and thin, like Miss Finch? He frowned. If she resembled Miss Finch in any way she would not be considered; even if she was Wenders' sister.

Then Sir Robert realised that he had forgotten to enquire as to Mrs. Brace's age. Apart from his mother's reference years ago that Wenders' sister was 'very young' her age was a mystery; but at least she was childless. Which was just as well, Sir Robert thought. Since under no circumstances would he have permitted any more children into his life. The twins were quite sufficient.

At that moment his ormolu clock struck six, and simultaneously there was a scuffling sound outside the door, accompanied by a sharp knock and it swung open. Immediately Edward bounded into the room, followed at a more sedate pace by Lucy.

'We've come to say night night and I's solly.'

Edward tumbled onto Sir Robert's lap, while Lucy snuggled up against one of his legs before waking Challenger to give him a hug. In their nightgowns and nightcaps they looked so vulnerable that the upheaval of the afternoon seemed to belong to another time, and Sir Robert spent the next few minutes listening contentedly to their chatter before relinquishing them to Hetty.

Unfortunately, this state of tranquillity only lasted until the following morning when, as Sir Robert and his friend Lord Merton were discussing yet another attack in the neighbourhood, there was a crashing sound from beneath the floor.

'Merciful heaven,' Lord Merton exclaimed. 'What was that?'

Without replying Sir Robert opened the door and stepped quickly into the hallway. From beyond the servants' entrance he could hear a considerable commotion, and as he hesitated Lucy descended the staircase accompanied by Hetty. He raised a questioning eyebrow at the nursemaid, who stared back nervously.

'I think it might be Master Edward, Sir Robert,' she murmured. 'He slipped away some time ago, and I've been trying to find him ever since.'

With a heavy sigh, Sir Robert refrained from reminding her that ensuring his nephew did not *slip away* was one of the prime reasons she was employed, and instead descended to the basement.

Accustomed to visiting the kitchen and scullery areas occasionally, since Sir Robert believed a master should be acquainted with all aspects of his dwelling, he was now gratified to see that the stone paved passageway was as spotless as on previous visits.

As he approached the noise it got louder, and when at last he reached the short flight of steps leading down into the kitchen, the vast room seemed to be full of people whose attention was directed at a small figure covered in something that looked suspiciously like blood. Large quantities of it were scattered across the floor, while Sir Robert's French chef, known to everyone as Monsieur, sobbed helplessly into his white overall.

Recognising his nephew through the mass of red Sir Robert stared aghast.

'Dear God,' he exclaimed.

At the sound of his voice everyone else jumped agitatedly, but Bridges the Head Groom held out a reassuring hand.

'It's jam, Sir Robert, only jam. Master Edward isn't hurt.'

Sir Robert picked his way carefully across the floor to where Edward was now sitting, trying to lick as much jam from his features as his small tongue could reach, while Challenger, who had followed his master down from the library was eagerly licking up the remaining mess from the floor.

As Sir Robert glanced helplessly around the room, a cacophony of voices tried to explain until Symons's voice boomed out, yet again, in explanation.

'Master Edward climbed unseen upon an upper shelf, Sir Robert, and knocked down a jar. Apparently, Monsieur required the jam for a confection he was preparing and as it was his last jar, hence his distress.'

'It's very nice,' Edward smiled up at Sir Robert. 'Would you like some, Uncle?'

Some hours later, having ensured that calm had once more returned to his household, Sir Robert sat in White's Club in St. James's discussing his problem with Lord Merton.

'How do you manage?' He asked wearily. 'You have four boys.'

'Ah, but I have a wife,' Lord Merton smiled. 'An indispensable addition to a household with young children; perhaps my dear Robert, you should ...'

'I know, I know,' Sir Robert waved a dismissive hand. 'But I refuse to marry in order to control a mischievous nephew.' He looked thoughtful. 'No, there is another way.'

2

'A lady, Sir Robert, we are to prepare for a *lady*?' Symons' ponderous bulk seemed to increase.

'Yes,' Sir Robert replied sharply. 'She is to be employed as the children's governess. So suitable accommodation should be arranged as near as possible to the nursery.'

'Is she to bring a maid, Sir Robert, and will there be anything of variety in eating matters? What am I to tell Monsieur, *on this occasion*?'

Sir Robert winced mentally as he remembered the crisis which had arisen on the twins' arrival. At that time his temperamental chef had been required to prepare, not only baby bottles of milk, but as they grew older, food suitable for infants. Sir Robert lifted his quizzing glass to his right eye and simultaneously raised an eyebrow, actions which indicated an audience was about to end even to so august a personage as Symons.

'As far as I am aware, Mrs. Brace will be unaccompanied, and if she has any particular likes or dislikes with regard to her meals, I am sure she will acquaint you with them on her arrival.'

The butler gave a stiff bow, and as the door closed behind him Sir Robert relaxed into his chair and glanced up at his mother's portrait for reassurance. Reynolds had painted her just before her wedding and her happiness was so apparent in her expression, Sir Robert felt that if the figure were to laugh suddenly it would not be unusual.

'You wanted me to have a lady in my life,' he murmured. 'So I suppose, in a way, you have achieved your ambition. Only I don't think she will be quite what you anticipated, even although you knew of her existence,' he added, with a chuckle.

The interview with Mrs. Brace had been swift and as far as Sir Robert was concerned, not altogether satisfactory. On being told that his sister was to be invited to attend at Grosvenor Square, Wenders had appeared hesitant.

'There is just one matter of which I should acquaint you, Sir Robert,' he had murmured diffidently. 'My sister has ventures.'

Alarmed, should his valet be referring to bouts of the vapours fashionable amongst certain young ladies of the day, Sir Robert looked questioningly at Wenders..

'Are you referring to her health, such as a tendency to swoon as a result, possibly, of her bereavement?'

'Dear me no, Sir Robert,' Wenders replied looking appalled. 'It is merely an interest in various matters. Such as the pursuance of an interest in ... horticulture.'

He pronounced the last word abruptly, as if it had only just occurred to him; but Sir Robert was not interested in Mrs. Brace's apparent addiction to gardening.

'Indeed, and to what extent will that affect her duties as a governess?'

'None at all, Sir Robert,' Wenders replied hurriedly. 'But I thought you should be aware of the fact.'

However addicted to her *ventures* Mrs. Brace was, Sir Robert never discovered because he forgot to ask; possibly because he was so surprised at the figure she presented. All his previous memories of Miss Finch's angular, unpleasant form vanished as soon as the rather plump personage of his future governess entered his drawing-room.

Apart from the fact that Mrs. Brace was approximately the same height as Miss Finch, and wore spectacles, her clothes and demeanour were a total contrast. Instead of being clad entirely in black, Mrs. Brace wore a light brown woollen pelisse covering a silk dress of the same colour. The necklines of both garments were trimmed with matching velvet, as were the brim of her otherwise plain straw bonnet and brown leather gloves.

Although the ensemble was an indication of taste rather than wealth, Sir Robert was acquainted enough with women's attire to realise that the garments had been tailored by a professional dressmaker. Mrs. Brace's manner also bore no resemblance to that of Miss Finch, for she smiled upon being introduced and her voice was gentle, without any of the latter's staccato tones.

As she had politely refused Sir Robert's offer of a chair, his impeccable manners forced him to remain standing during the interview, a situation he found rather daunting, especially as Mrs. Brace appeared to be entirely at her ease and, apparently, expected him to conduct the conversation.

The preliminary introductions having been completed Wenders had taken his leave, and somewhat at a loss as to how to proceed, Sir Robert had first thanked Mrs. Brace for attending and then, after mentioning vaguely that his mother had been aware that Wenders had a sister, asked with some hesitancy why she had left her previous post.

'I had completed all I wished to do,' she had replied. 'There is only so much one can teach young children; and I do not consider myself able to teach beyond the year of eleven.'

'But surely since you were at a school there must have been other younger children taking the place of those who had progressed?'

'Possibly, but I had completed all I wished to do,' she had repeated.

'And you obtained that post after your very sad bereavement?' Sir Robert had enquired sympathetically, thinking perhaps she might care to refer to her late husband. But instead of replying verbally Mrs. Brace just gave a polite nod.

At this response Sir Robert had hesitated. Although he had no wish to broach sad memories, he now realised he should have pursued in more detail her past life and experience, but there had been something implacable about her stance and manner that made him suspect that if he questioned her too deeply, she would have refused the position. Her monosyllabic responses became frustrating, so in an effort to arouse her Sir Robert had concentrated on her future charges.

'Although the children are still very young,' he explained, 'I wish them to improve their reading, and as I understand you are conversant with the French language, I would like it to be included in their studies. And I would like Lucy to participate in all her brother is taught. I do not believe female education should be restricted to painting and pianoforte' Again Mrs. Brace had nodded in apparent understanding as Sir Robert, by now eager to bring the interview to a close had struggled on. 'Apart from French, and whenever you consider it opportune, I would also like them to have a knowledge of Latin and Greek.'

As he finished speaking he thought he detected an expression of surprise in Mrs. Brace's face, and gratified to have aroused some reaction, however slight, he had asked if she would like to meet her future charges.

'I think not, if you are agreeable, Sir Robert,' she had replied, her expression suddenly serious. 'A very brief meeting with a stranger can disturb a child. I would prefer to meet them knowing our encounter was to be permanent. That is, of course, if you consider I am suitable for the position,' she had added with a questioning glance.

Relieved that their encounter was nearing its end, Sir Robert had waved a reassuring hand.

'Indeed, I am pleased to offer you the post to commence whenever you are able.'

He had then given her a slight bow, and had been about to ring the hand bell for Wenders when he had realised she was looking at him expectantly.

'Thank you, Sir Robert, but may I enquire as to the remuneration?'

He had stared at her uncomprehendingly for some seconds, before realising what she meant. Although the welfare of his servants had always concerned him, Sir Robert had no idea as to the wages any of them earned. It had always been his practice to leave this aspect of their employment to be supervised by his London steward, William Best.

Consequently, he had regarded Mrs. Brace in something of a panic until, possibly aware of his predicament, she had smiled in apparent understanding.

'If it is of any assistance, Sir Robert, Miss Trent, a friend who is engaged in Lord Haversham's establishment, receives twelve pounds a year.'

Sir Robert had been shocked. The Havershams were amongst the richest landowners in Kent, and lived and entertained lavishly. They also had five children, all under the age of ten years, and had always boasted that they were more than generous to their retainers. Sir Robert had looked contemplatively at his new governess.

'And does Miss Trent have any assistance with her duties?'

'No, she is responsible entirely for all the children's education and activities.'

'I see. Then I think a remuneration of sixteen pounds a year is called for, if that is to your satisfaction?'

If he had anticipated another reaction he was disappointed, for when she replied both Mrs. Brace's expression and voice had been unemotional.

'Thank you, Sir Robert, that will be most satisfactory.'

On the day of her arrival, Sir Robert returned home from a prolonged luncheon engagement to discover Mrs. Brace had established her small domain in the day and night nurseries, and was already engaged in supervising the twins' supper.

Sir Robert looked enquiringly at Wenders, as the latter assisted him to dress for an engagement at Almacks that evening.

'I believe all is progressing well, Sir Robert.' The valet gave one of his rare smiles. 'Mrs. Brace appears to have been accepted with much pleasure. Even Mr. Symons and Monsieur have not indicated any form of discontent.'

'Good Lord,' Sir Robert exclaimed. Then remembering to whom he was speaking added, 'I beg your pardon, Wenders, but your sister must have remarkable powers.'

'She is very adaptable, Sir Robert,' Wenders replied with a satisfied expression.

'Indeed, and would I be a welcome goodnight guest if I were to proceed upstairs? It would not be considered an intrusion?'

'I believe, Sir Robert, you are eagerly awaited.'

Despite Wenders' encouragement, Sir Robert was still slightly apprehensive as he approached the flight of stairs leading to the nursery but he was soon reassured on hearing the murmur of a woman's voice instead of the usual din. Peeping into the large white-painted bedroom, he discovered Mrs. Brace seated before the fire in the largest armchair with a twin tucked in on either side of her, while at her feet Challenger lounged comfortably.

Both children were so absorbed in what she was saying that neither of them noticed Sir Robert as he stood listening at the door. The story appeared to concern a kitten which had got lost, but at the moment the mother cat was about to look into the box in which the kitten was trapped, Mrs. Brace closed the book. The twins immediately began to protest, but she shook her head.

'If you know the end of the story today, you won't want any more tomorrow. And it's more exciting to wonder, isn't it?'

Lucy looked doubtful, but by that time Edward had seen his uncle and bounded across to Sir Robert, yelling excitedly.

'We like Mrs. Brace, she's nice.'

Swinging him up into his arms, Sir Robert gave Edward a hug then did the same to Lucy. As he did so he glanced about the room. Although it appeared as usual, he noted that fresh flowers had been placed on the two wooden chests, and the twins' bed now had new pretty white hangings and covers.

Mrs. Brace arose, and after giving him a brief, but not unfriendly nod, ushered the children towards the bed. After bidding them goodnight, Sir Robert retreated into the corridor and waited until she emerged.

'I have made one or two alterations, Sir Robert,' she said closing the door behind her. 'I trust they are to your liking?'

'Indeed yes, and I hope you are making full use of Hetty. She is a simple girl but very willing.'

Before Mrs. Brace could reply, there was a resounding sound like an explosion from somewhere outside the house.

24

Immediately the twins could be heard crying out, and Mrs. Brace hurriedly returned to the nursery, while Sir Robert proceeded swiftly downstairs to the main hall where William Best, and Radcliff the porter, were standing at the open front door.

'Sounded like someone firing a musket, Sir Robert,' Radcliff exclaimed. 'It came from the other side of the square.'

'This makes five happenings in two weeks,' Best declared. 'And there was the man who frightened Millie the other night. What's going on, Sir Robert?'

'I cannot imagine, but I think it wise for the servants to remain indoors after dark, no matter how urgent the cause for them to leave the house.'

'Will you be going out tonight, Sir Robert?' Radcliff asked, looking concerned.

'Yes, I am promised to Lord and Lady Merton at Almacks, but I will ensure that I return earlier than usual. I find these disturbances most troubling. It might be wise if we were to progress to Hawton Hall earlier than is usual this year. I will give it some thought.'

His coach arrived in King Street at the same time as that of his friend Lord Randall, and the two men entered the Assembly Rooms together. In Sir Robert's opinion the building, regarded by the fashionable world as the epitome of elegance, survived because of its reputation as a Marriage Mart, and he considered the vast ballroom's gilt columns and gas lit cut glass candelabra extremely vulgar.

He had also little respect for the patronesses who, far from being the paragons of virtue they appeared to be, were known to Sir Robert as women with dubious pasts who juggled their lovers with the agility of experts.

In an atmosphere too warm for comfort, the two men eased their way through acres of men clad in velvet coats and kerseymere breeches, and endless queues of women all clad in muslin and organza. When they finally reached the dining room, it was to find the Mertons and their other guests already installed at a table. Only Sir Robert's warm regard for his friend, and the knowledge that Lady Merton genuinely enjoyed Almacks, enabled him to tolerate the unappetising food and the ratafia and orgeat which were the only drinks available.

Predictably, as soon as greetings had been exchanged, the conversation centred on the recent violent incidents, the last of which had distressed Alice Merton greatly.

'I have told David that we should remove to Ashworth until we are assured that these terrible happenings are no more; and especially since the disappearance of Meggie.'

'Gracious,' Lady Baberstock, one of their guests, declared. 'Disappeared, is that possible?'

Lord Merton laughed. 'Apparently so, and I am convinced it is a matter of the heart. Although Alice will insist the matter has more relevance.'

'Indeed it has,' Lady Merton declared. 'Meggie was a quiet, shy girl, who rarely stirred from the house. It was most odd, for she departed without a character to present. So no one will employ her, and I cannot imagine where she can have gone. I wanted the constabulary to be informed but David seems to think it will do more harm than good.'

'Possibly so,' Lady Baberstock replied. 'But the sooner these terrible occurrences are solved and the perpetrators apprehended, the sooner we shall be able to walk the streets again in safety.'

'I fear that is some time away, Lady Baberstock,' Lord Clive, another guest, replied. 'The Bow Street Runners seem unable to apprehend anyone, although they have been roaming the area for over a week past. I read today in *The Morning Post* that desecraters have been at their depraved activities once again, violating graveyards in both Hackney and Stepney village.' He frowned. 'I am convinced that until we have a proper group of people dedicated only to solving crime, there will never be complete harmony in this city.'

Lord Randall laughed sardonically. 'And from where pray, does one select such a force? Certainly not from the present iniquitous group of men who constitute our policing officers, and City Patrol.'

'But surely now that those corrupt police officers, George Vaughan and Robert Mackay, are no longer at large, a lesson has been learned, and any man selected will know his duties?' Lord Merton protested; only to be interrupted by Lady Cooper, Lady Merton's sister.

'I am of the opinion that only complete gas lighting of all the streets will alleviate crime,' she said firmly.

'The expense would be prohibitive,' Sir Robert murmured. 'And a number of crimes are committed where it would be impossible to place street lighting.'

'Apart from the recent ones,' Lady Merton added before turning to her husband. 'I truly believe dearest, 'tis better if we left London until the end of summer.'

'But we cannot let such hooligans deprive us of the season's enjoyments,' Lord Merton declared sharply. 'No, such concerns are unnecessary I assure you, my dear.'

Lord Merton's manners towards his wife were usually impeccable, and his rebuttal surprised Sir Robert since it was so completely out of character. His reaction was obviously shared by Lady Merton. After looking sharply at her husband she arose from her chair, and ignoring the gentlemen, turned with a taut expression towards her female companions.

'I declare, ladies,' she announced coldly. 'Despite my husband's comments, we are at this moment being denied an enjoyment, namely that new innovation the waltz. Come, let us to the ballroom, and can I persuade you to escort us, Lord Baberstock?'

'No persuasion is required I assure you, Lady Merton,' he replied, and gallantly offering her his arm swept her away, followed by everyone except Sir Robert, and Lord Randall.

'As Madeleine has not accompanied you this evening, I trust she is not unwell?' Sir Robert said, as he watched his departing friends being slowly absorbed into the crowd of dancers.

Lord Randall shrugged. 'Not so far as I am aware, but you know how she is. Lives almost permanently in a state of the vapours. Something to do with a truculent maid, I think, was her excuse this evening. Merton was rather sharp with Alice, wasn't he?' Not wishing to discuss his friend's behaviour, Sir Robert merely nodded as Lord Randall continued, 'What say you we go on to Whites? I am deuced bored here, and there's not a female in sight I would care to address.'

Sir Robert hesitated a moment, before replying. 'Forgive me, George, but you lost a deal at the tables on Saturday. Do you think it wise we should go?'

Lord Randall's lips tightened slightly. 'You may be my friend, Robert, but I'll not take such language from anyone. What I do with my money is my own affair. Now, will you accompany me or not?'

'I think not tonight,' Sir Robert replied quietly. 'My duty is with our hostess.' He stood up and edged his way around the table. As he did so he placed a hand lightly on Lord Randall's shoulder.

'My apologies, George, it was but friendly meant.'

Lord Randall sighed. 'I know, I know, but you're aware how it is with me, Robert. The tables seem to have a deadly appeal.'

Later, having danced with Lady Merton and the other ladies of the party, Sir Robert excused himself and called for his carriage. Relaxing comfortably into the upholstery he was considering the day's unusual events when, on entering St. James's Street, he caught sight of George Randall staggering down the steps of White's Club towards a waiting coach.

Sir Robert watched in concern, and would have ordered his coachman to stop and assist, if it had not been for Lord Randall's admonishment earlier. So instead Sir Robert watched helplessly his friend's undignified attempts to enter the coach, eventually succeeding only with the assistance of his coachman and a passing stranger.

Sir Robert had known both Randall and Merton since their schooldays, and the three men had been firm friends ever since. But whereas David Merton was reputed to be a steady caring man, who adored his wife and sons and tended to his estate responsibilities, George Randall had acquired a reputation as a gambler, whose every penny slipped through his fingers like water from a jug.

This had not always been the case. Prior to 1815 Lord Randall had been regarded as a reliable man with a happy and contented married life; but since England's victory at Waterloo two years previously, for no accountable reason he had commenced a life of debauchery, which had shocked society and driven his wife into ill health.

The resultant series of arguments and accusations had degenerated into a morose, unhappy domestic situation, which had affected their son as much as themselves. With the result that nine-year old Edgar, after enduring two years of upheaval, had grown to believe that such behaviour was a normal part of family life.

Puzzled by this abrupt change in his friend's personality, Sir Robert had attempted to discover the reason, but all his efforts were met with such evasiveness and annoyance, he had decided the only way he could assist George Randall was to continue their friendship without further interference.

Perhaps it was the result of seeing his friend in such a distressing state that Sir Robert realised he had not derived much pleasure from the evening's pursuits, but on arriving back at his house all was so peaceful, he retired feeling considerably happier and more relaxed.

It is possible he might not have felt so sanguine had he witnessed the masked black-clad figure climb out of a window at the top of his house, before making its way across the roof tops.

3

Despite the tranquillity that now pervaded his home, Sir Robert found his days rather unfulfilling. Although he would never have admitted it, the domestic calm seemed to have deprived his life of a certain diversity which, he now realised, he had enjoyed.

Since acquiring the age of mobility the twins had brought havoc to the previously staid bachelor establishment, and although Sir Robert knew their lives were being administered to more professionally than in the past, he missed Edward's impetuous ways and Lucy's wide-eyed curiosity.

Sometimes, when the silence was almost disconcerting, he would climb up to the nursery and peep in to see if all was well. Reassured by what he saw, but aware that he must not intrude, he would return reluctantly to the library, leaving the twins seated at their little desks doing something industrious with pieces of chalk, while Mrs. Brace moved from one desk to the other quietly encouraging them.

Another aspect of the twins' behaviour that Sir Robert found difficult to accept was their good manners. Edward no long flung himself at his uncle to be hugged, nor did

Lucy snuggle into his chair; as *Good-nights* were now conducted in their bedroom in the presence of Mrs. Brace.

He also missed driving with them in his curricle; despite the number of times Bridges had been forced to drag Edward back onto his seat from a possible demise beneath the wheels.

Sir Robert tried to reassure himself that he was being ridiculous, and that his life had improved since the governess's arrival, but the strange nagging ache would not be dismissed. Which was why, two weeks later he requested the twins presence alone in his library. Walter looked at his employer in surprise.

'Without Mrs. Brace, Sir Robert?'

'That is what I said,' Sir Robert replied, trying not to sound peremptory.

Some minutes later the twins entered with wide welcoming smiles, and Sir Robert extended his arms. Immediately, they ran forward to be hugged and he swung them up, one in each arm, before lowering them gently to the floor.

'Mrs. Brace said you wanted to see us, Uncle Robert?' Lucy looked up questioningly.

Sir Robert returned to his chair and lifted her onto his knee.

'I just wanted to know whether you were enjoying your lessons,' he explained, hoping he did not sound as uncertain as he felt.

'Oh, yes, Uncle Robert,' Edward declared enthusiastically. 'I can count up to twenty now, and we're learning the alphabet as well. And we like Mrs. Brace, don't we, Lucy?'

'Oh, yes, Uncle Robert.' She nodded her head vigorously. 'We like Mrs. Brace, she's very nice.'

'But we love you, Uncle Robert,' Edward interrupted, giving Sir Robert's left leg a hug.

Any concerns Sir Robert may have felt about the children's feelings towards him vanished, and it was with some emotion that he guided them gently towards the door. As he opened it, he was disconcerted to find Mrs. Brace sitting on the far side of the hall reading a book. She looked up with a smile.

'It is such a lovely day today, Sir Robert, have I your permission to take the children for a drive?'

Gratified that she had considered it necessary to ask, Sir Robert nodded.

'Of course, do whatever you think is best for the children, and it is not necessary to obtain my agreement,' he added, returning her smile.

'I thought I would enquire, in view of the recent disturbances,' she replied.

'I had forgotten the troubles.' Sir Robert frowned for a moment, then an idea occurred to him, and he glanced rather warily at her. 'Instead of taking the carriage, perhaps you would agree to me driving the children in my curricle. They have not been out with me for some time, and please do accompany us if you so wish,' he added, hurriedly.

'Thank you, Sir Robert, that is a kind thought.' She gave a polite nod. 'Edward has told me many times how much he enjoys driving with you, and I would consider it a pleasure to accompany them. Shall we go upstairs, children, to prepare for the outing?'

For the first time since their governess's arrival, the house rang with the twins' whoops of joy, as they followed Mrs. Brace up the stairs.

Feeling more contented than he had for some days, Sir Robert was about to follow when he noticed Mrs. Brace's book lying on her chair. Wondering idly what branch of literature occupied her, he picked it up, and was astonished to discover it was a medical manual, containing explicit pictures of dismembered bodies.

Thinking that perhaps it was a book she had borrowed out of morbid curiosity, Sir Robert looked at the flyleaf, but written in neat script was her name *Amanda Wenders*. Shocked, and not wishing any other members of his staff to see it, Sir Robert slipped it into his waistcoat before continuing to his bedroom, where Wenders was busily engaged in laying out his master's outdoor apparel.

'Bridges is preparing the horses, Sir Robert,' he murmured, as he eased his master deftly into his coat. 'And the children and Mrs. Brace will be awaiting you in the hall.'

Taking advantage of the governess's name having being mentioned, Sir Robert waved a hand towards her book now lying on his bureau.

'I believe that belongs to Mrs. Brace. Perhaps you would kindly return it to her.'

'Of course, Sir Robert,' Wenders replied, picking up the manual without opening it.

Intrigued, Sir Robert stood in the doorway hat in hand, as he asked: 'Are you aware of what that book contains?'

'I fear I do, Sir Robert,' Wenders replied with a dejected expression. 'It is one of my sister's ventures. Not, I hasten to add that she indulges in such practices herself. She is just interested,' he concluded, looking even sadder.

'But she must have been quite young, when she first read it? I see the name on the fly-leaf is that of her family, rather than her husband.'

Wenders' despondent expression increased. 'Indeed, Sir Robert, her interests have always been somewhat enigmatic.'

Disturbed that he had possibly assigned the lives of his small relatives into the care of someone whose leisure hours were spent reading about dismembered cadavers, Sir Robert descended to the hallway considerably confused.

Despite the twins' obvious enjoyment, Sir Robert remained in a distracted state for most of the drive; which was possibly why he was not aware of the interest directed at him and his passengers as his carriage progressed through the park.

At last, having cast a number of surreptitious glances at Mrs. Brace's innocuous figure Sir Robert decided to consider her choice of reading matter just slightly eccentric, and delivered his charges back home amidst loud demands from the twins for another ride very soon.

That same evening, Sir Robert was engaged to join a party of friends at the Covent Garden Theatre for the first performance in English of *Don Giovanni*, an event which the fashionable world had been anticipating for some months. Although disappointed that on this occasion, yet another of Lady Randall's indispositions would mean that neither she nor her husband, would be present, Sir Robert, a great admirer of Mozart, anticipated an evening of considerable enjoyment.

It was as he was about to descend the stairs to the hallway that Mrs. Brace appeared on the landing looking concerned.

'Forgive me for being intrusive, Sir Robert,' she said. 'But I understand you will be travelling through town this evening and if this is the case, may I suggest Rivers takes great care when returning to Grosvenor Square. There has been another disturbance, this time in Hamilton Place. A carriage was attacked, and as on previous occasions the assailant was seen to be wearing a mask.'

Before Sir Robert could reply, or ask her from where she had obtained her information, she had given him a brief nod and departed up the nursery staircase.

The opera was superb, and the supper afterwards at the home of Sir Robert's friends the Mancasters, was a perfect end to an enchanting evening.

During the meal the opera was discussed animatedly, but afterwards in the drawing room when the gentlemen had once more joined the ladies, Lady Baberstock leaned towards Sir Robert with a smile.

'I was indeed gratified to see in what excellent health the children appeared this morning. In the park in your curricle,' she added, in response to Sir Robert's puzzled expression.

'Of course,' he said, smiling. 'I had forgotten. It was Mrs. Brace's suggestion that they took the air.'

'Mrs. Brace?' Lady Baberstock looked at him enquiringly, while the other ladies exchanged glances.

Aware suddenly that everyone appeared to be listening to their conversation, Sir Robert frowned.

'She is the children's governess,' he explained, rather stiffly. 'I decided they were of an age when such a personage was advisable.'

'How very wise,' Lady Baberstock murmured. 'Life would be unsupportable without their assistance, would it not, Lady Merton?'

'Indeed, it would,' Lady Merton replied. 'Why, if our dear Miss Machine were to leave I cannot think how we would exist. Life would be impossible, would it not, my love?' she added to her husband.

He laughed. 'It would certainly be less tolerable, so we must hope she does not decide to depart like the hapless Meggie. Of whom, we have yet heard nothing,' he added, in answer to questioning glances. 'But Robert, why did you not tell us of your new acquisition? And from where did you acquire her? Brace, you say, now from what part of the country would such a name originate?'

'I have no idea, and she was recommended,' Sir Robert replied briefly, having no intention of involving his valet. Then he remembered Mrs. Brace's choice of reading matter.

'You have lauded Miss Machine's attributes on many occasions,' he declared. 'But may I enquire does she have ventures?'

'Ventures? What in heaven's name are those?' Lord Mancaster exclaimed while everyone exchanged surprised glances.

'Er. ... books,' Sir Robert replied.

'Of course, she has books,' Lady Merton said somewhat testily. 'She's a governess.'

'May I enquire what kind of books?' Sir Robert enquired.

'My dear fellow,' Lord Merton declared before his wife could reply. 'Why not ask your governess what she reads? Surely her choice of reading matter is of more importance than that of Miss Machine. And anyway they probably read entirely different books, 'cause none of these women are the same. They're all different, don't you know.'

'Who are?' Lord Baberstock, who had imbibed rather unwisely, peered vaguely at the speaker.

'Governesses, but how did we come to discuss such a topic?' Lord Mancaster declared. 'Come now, the evening is yet young. Let's to more interesting matters.'

'If you want something more interesting,' Lord Baberstock declared. 'Then here's one. Have you heard that Napoleon is believed to be dying?'

'Never,' Lord Merton declared, with a laugh. 'The man's invulnerable. He'll last forever.'

'If he does, at least we can be sure it will always be on St. Helena,' Lord Mancaster replied. 'There's no way he'll ever be able to leave that island.'

'Not unless some besotted fool tried to aid him,' Sir Robert said wryly.

'Even then, it is well in excess of a thousand miles from the African coast,' Lord Merton declared, emphatically. 'No, I think we can rest assured such an attempt will never be made.'

Lord Mancaster raised his eyebrows in apparent surprise. 'You sound very positive, my friend. Have you studied the subject?'

'On the contrary,' Lord Merton began somewhat heatedly, only to be interrupted by Lady Mancaster returning from the hallway, where she had been bidding farewell to some of her other guests.

'My dear,' she said, addressing her husband, 'it is now past one o'clock and such late hours are not wise at the present time. The Bassengers have just left us, and I fear we must bid farewell to our remaining guests, loath though I am so to do.'

As if to confirm her words, the Mertons were already preparing to leave and soon all the guests were boarding their carriages.

Despite his enjoyment of the opera, Sir Robert drove home feeling dissatisfied without understanding the reason. He had certainly been irritated by Lord Mancaster's flippant dismissal of the subject of governesses and their reading matter, but such a minor incident should not have made him feel so downcast. Also David Merton's unexpected outburst regarding Napoleon puzzled Sir Robert. It was almost as if he had resented Lord Mancaster's reference to the Emperor which, Sir Robert thought, was unreasonable. Despite two years having elapsed since Napoleon's incarceration on St. Helena, he was still a popular topic of conversation, which was not surprising, considering the havoc he had once perpetrated on Europe.

Sir Robert was still meditating when the carriage stopped and Newsome opened the door. Descending to the street, Sir Robert was shaken abruptly out of his reverie by the unexpected sight of Symons standing beside Radcliff at the open front door. Since the butler would never have lowered himself to accompany the porter on his duties, such a sight did not bode good news and Sir Robert felt his stomach contract at the expression on the porter's face.

'The children ...?' he gasped.

Symons shook his head. 'No no, Sir Robert, rest assured they are well. It is Mrs. Brace. She's been attacked.'

'The devil she has,' Sir Robert exclaimed in horror. 'Is she badly hurt?'

'No, but badly bruised, Sir Robert,' Wenders murmured as he stepped from behind the open door. 'I have taken the liberty of sending for the physician to tend her, and trust that this meets with your approval.'

'But of course, and thank God it's no worse.' Sir Robert waved agitatedly at Radcliff. 'And close the door, man, and why do you stare so? Has something else happened?'

'Not here, Sir Robert, but out in the east of the city,' Symons replied, his expression indicating that such an area was as alien to him as were those inhabited by the wilder of the jungle tribes.

'It's in Stepney village, Sir Robert,' Radcliff explained. 'Another grave's been dug up. Walter's brother's just sent word.'

'Merciful heaven, whatever next?' Sir Robert shook his head. 'But Stepney village is a long way away. So calm yourselves everyone, and take a draught. It will lighten your fears if nothing else.'

A chorus of effusive thanks followed this remark, and then everyone seemed to melt into the fabric of the building, leaving only Radcliff and Wenders standing with Sir Robert in the hall.

'Now.' He stared hard at his valet. 'What of Mrs. Brace? How did it happen.?

'I fear she wished to take the evening air, Sir Robert,' Wenders replied, looking apologetic.

'The evening air, for pity's sake the woman's mad,' Sir Robert expostulated. 'After all the attacks recently and her own warning to me to take care; surely she realised the danger? Could she not have just opened a window?'

Wenders nodded without replying, and seeing his distressed expression Sir Robert remembered that it was his valet's sister they were discussing, and he waved a conciliatory hand.

'No matter, I was concerned for her welfare, that is all. But I shall advise her not to be so foolhardy in future. If she desires to leave the house, she must take one of the footmen with her, and I must visit her. Tomorrow perhaps, a visit will not unduly distress her?'

'I am assured, Sir Robert, that a visit from you would be most welcome.'

'Then so be it, at eleven o'clock.'

With an unexpected feeling of anticipation, Sir Robert entered his library where after considerable thought he decided that the most sensible thing to do, in view of the continued disturbances, was to leave London earlier than was customary. The Season was almost over, and Hawton's country air and pursuits would be far healthier for the children than the life they were now leading in the city.

But later, having decided to retire, he hesitated on reaching the landing. Everything seemed peaceful and he knew there was no reason to be disturbed, but despite himself he needed reassurance. So he climbed up to the twins' bedroom and peeped inside.

Lucy lay in tranquil repose between undisturbed sheets, her head slightly turned on the pillow and her left arm encircling her doll; but on the other side of the bed Edward's covers were awry leaving his feet exposed.

Sir Robert tiptoed across the room and gently replaced the bedding around his small nephew, before tucking him in. As he did so he thought he heard a sound and turned quickly, but the door connecting the twins' room with that of Mrs. Brace was closed. So he decided it must have been his imagination.

The following morning, as soon as Wenders entered the bedchamber Sir Robert advised him of his decision to leave London.

'Very well, Sir Robert, to Hawton Hall on Friday,' Wenders nodded his head. 'I will advise Symons and Mrs. Brace.'

'No, I will tell her,' Sir Robert replied firmly. 'When I see her this morning.'

'Very well, Sir Robert,' Wenders replied with a marked lack of enthusiasm..

Before visiting the governess, Sir Robert paid a visit to the day nursery where he found the twins, supervised by Hetty, scribbling on a blackboard pinned to the wall.

As he entered all three looked up before the twins, with cries of: 'Uncle, Uncle,' dropped their chalks and dashed up to be hugged.

'Mrs. Brace told me to let them draw, Sir Robert,' Hetty said with a curtsy. 'She thought they would enjoy doing that.'

With a twin in each arm Sir Robert tried to decipher the squiggly white shapes on the blackboard.

'What are they drawing? Boxes?'

At this, Edward wriggled in apparent outrage. 'No no, Uncle, mine's not a box, it's an elepthump.'

'And mine's a tiger,' Lucy declared indignantly.

Sir Robert lowered them both to the floor. 'Have you ever seen a drawing of an elephant or a tiger?'

'No,' they replied in unison. 'And it's an elepthump, Uncle. An elepTHUMP!'

Vanquished, Sir Robert retreated to seek out Mrs. Brace.

He found her sitting in her parlour, wearing a loose fitting garment of white lawn and with her feet supported by a footstool. Possibly because her hair was hanging about her shoulders, and she was in a state of mild deshabille, Sir Robert hesitated at the entrance. But when she indicated a nearby chair he approached, only to exclaim with shock at the sight of her bandaged left hand and arm, and the bruise which covered the majority of her left cheek.

She smiled wanly. 'I fear I am somewhat incommoded, Sir Robert, and must apologise for this disruption to your household. Especially after my warning to you.'

Very concerned, he shook his head. 'Not at all, you could in no way have envisaged this, and my household will continue as before. It is your health and recovery that are paramount; but how did it happen? I have received only the barest details.'

'I was walking along the road, but a few yards from the house, when someone ... I know not whether it was a man or woman, sprang at me from an entry, and laid me low. The physician has assured me that no bones are broken, but I caught my arm in falling, and it bled slightly hence the bandage. But I think if I can rest for say a day more, I shall be fit to resume my duties on Friday,' she concluded, her voice sounding suddenly weaker.

Sir Robert shook his head. 'No, you must not consider returning to work before next week. The twins' education will not suffer if their governess is absent for so short a time; but there is another matter of which I wish to acquaint you. Because of the recent disturbances, and your unfortunate encounter, I have decided to depart for Hawton Hall, my estate in Hampshire, earlier than has been my practice in the past. There are but two weeks of the Summer Season remaining, and the weather has been so cold and inclement this past month, if it continues outdoor pursuits will be unappealing. I am therefore making arrangements for us to leave on Saturday, by which time I anticipate you will have recovered sufficiently enough for the journey.'

Mrs. Brace frowned and appeared about to speak, but then instead turned her head and glanced out of the window.

Sir Robert arose from his chair. 'I will not tire you by remaining further. There will be nothing for you to prepare, as Hetty will see to the children's needs, and I will arrange for one of the parlour maids to attend you.' Then a thought occurred to him. 'You will, of course, travel with us in my travelling coach. It is large enough for you to occupy an entire side, which will make the journey more tolerable, and we will not exhaust ourselves. I shall send ahead to The Talbot Inn at Ripley for the night. It is a fair hostelry, and I have always found it comfortable.'

On Thursday, after London society had been informed of Sir Robert's plans in the social column of a newspaper, Symons knocked on the library door to announce Lord Randall. Sir Robert greeted him in some surprise, since he had assumed his friend would be attending the Newmarket races.

'Deuced good of you to see me, Robert,' Lord Randall murmured, lowering himself into a proffered chair. 'Truth is, I'm seeking a favour, and if you deny me I'll not take it amiss, but I'd be grateful for your compliance.'

'My dear fellow, what is it? You know I'll always help in any way I can.'

'It's the lad,' Lord Randall said diffidently. 'Would you take him with you? He's no bother, always quiet too quiet really, and he'll behave himself, always has. Y'see it's Madeleine, she's very cast down at the moment, and I think it's bad for the boy. I found him in tears yesterday.' Lord Randall's voice became suddenly thick with emotion.

'Didn't know what to do. Never seen him like that. Made me wonder how often it's happened. I suppose I ought to send him to school, but he'd never last a day at Eton, or Harrow. He's so thin, he'd never be able ...'

'Say no more,' Sir Robert interrupted shocked by his friend's distraught manner. 'My dear friend of course I'll take him. Do not trouble yourself; the boy will come with us. It's of no consequence, just have him ready on Saturday morning by, say eight o'clock, and we will collect him on our way out of town.'

'And your new governess, she'll not object?' Lord Randall looked suddenly wary. 'In view of her condition?'

'Certainly not,' Sir Robert replied forgetting to enquire, in his eagerness to reassure his friend, how Lord Randall knew about Mrs. Brace's injuries.

But now reminded of her existence, he repeated his invitation with an assurance he did not feel. He had overlooked Mrs. Brace when making his impulsive offer, and it was with some trepidation that he sought her out later.

'He's just nine years,' he explained. 'And I would not have exposed you to this added responsibility, especially in view of your present state of health, if it had not been an urgent case. He's a quiet child. I have met him occasionally, and found him to be very biddable. I think you will find him a docile charge.'

Mrs. Brace smiled. Her health appeared to have improved considerably since Sir Robert's last visit, and she was now sitting with the twins in the day nursery reading them a story.

'I have yet to meet a docile charge,' she said with a light laugh. 'And you say his name is Edgar?'

'Yes, he is Lord Randall's only child,' Sir Robert explained, and was then surprised by a sudden change in her expression. But her face quickly resumed its customary calm appearance, and she nodded in apparent understanding.

Some hours later, after the twins were in bed and Sir Robert was safely ensconced in his library, Mrs. Brace summoned her brother. Have apparently satisfied himself that the other servants were fully occupied elsewhere, Wenders joined her, and after locking her bedroom door, carefully unwound the bandage on her left arm, revealing a gash which stretched from above her left wrist to below her elbow.

4

The journey to Ripley was accomplished at a somewhat slower pace than was customary for Sir Robert's coaches. As Hawton Hall was always kept fully staffed, the only servants travelling from London, apart from Wenders and Hetty, were Rivers Newsome, Sam Bridges, and two junior grooms plus, on this occasion, two out-riders, who Sir Robert had decided to employ in view of the recent disturbances.

He had insisted on an early departure, hoping this would result in the twins falling asleep thus ensuring Mrs. Brace's travelling would pass as calmly as possible.

The ruse worked, and the twins were soon nestling in his arms while Mrs. Brace, spread across the opposite side of the coach, dozed intermittently. Only Edgar wedged at the side of the coach appeared uneasy. Concerned that he might be feeling homesick, Sir Robert gave him an encouraging smile to which the boy's mouth twitched slightly in response.

Apart from a whispered thanks on being lifted into the coach by his father, Edgar had said nothing since leaving London. Sir Robert suspected his subdued and nervous manner was due to him leaving his home which, although not the happiest of places, was at least somewhere the child knew and understood.

The coach gave a sharp lurch, and Sir Robert glanced nervously at Mrs. Brace but she smiled back reassuringly.

'Your coach is indeed well sprung, Sir Robert. I have never before travelled in such comfort.'

'Thank you, but there is much for which we must thank Mr. Obadiah Elliott,' Sir .Robert replied with a quiet laugh. 'This was but a normal coach when purchased, but I had it redesigned to withstand all forms of roadway, and to accommodate a greater number as you can see.'

At that moment the coachman's horn was heard announcing the approaching toll-gate, and the twins awoke demanding to know where they were. As the horses were pulled in Mrs. Brace declined to move, but everyone else descended, and after ensuring Hetty would attend to the twins' needs Sir Robert strolled out of the yard.

They were now in the country and green fields and woodland stretched as far as he could see. Revelling in the scene he drew a deep breath, before murmuring to himself, 'This is England at her very best.'

'Yes, sir, that's what my Papa always says.'

Staring down in surprise Sir Robert found Edgar, apparently equally absorbed, and he placed his right hand lightly on the boy's shoulders.

'And do you travel much into the country with your Papa?'

'Not any more, sir,' Edgar gave a little sigh. 'Not since he became so very busy with his work.'

Sir Robert frowned. Gambling was not a pursuit he would have described as *work*, but reluctant to comment he guided Edgar towards the local well, from which the servants and horses were now drinking.

'Let us take a cup of water to Mrs. Brace,' Sir Robert suggested. 'Would you like to carry it?'

Edgar nodded shyly but accepted the proffered cup with enthusiasm, before carrying it very carefully towards the coach. As he reached the vehicle, Mrs. Brace leaned somewhat precariously out of the door.

'Thank you so very much, Edgar,' she declared. 'That is most kind.'

Apparently overwhelmed by the unexpected praise Edgar blushed heavily while Sir Robert, aware that at any moment Mrs. Brace might lose her balance, reached out an arm and pushed her gently back onto her seat.

The action took no more than three seconds to accomplish, but it left Sir Robert feeling strangely embarrassed and he turned hastily away to hide his confusion.

The remaining miles to Ripley, and their night at The Talbot Inn, passed uneventfully. The twins, being so exhausted by the journey, fell asleep immediately after their supper; and having confirmed with Wenders that Mrs. Brace had everything she required, Sir Robert retreated to his own room where he spent the remainder of the evening reading.

Perhaps it was due to this self-indulgence that he felt somewhat guilty the following morning on enquiring whether everyone had slept well.

'I believe so, Sir Robert,' Mrs. Brace replied, as the travelling coach manoeuvred its way out of the inn yard. 'At least, Edgar and I slept very well, and Hetty told me the twins did not awaken until she arose herself.'

The carriages continued to bowl along at speed, and they were soon on the outskirts of Hawton village which bordered the estate. Situated in the southern precincts of Hampshire, it was fifteen miles from the coast, and surrounded by well cultivated farmland and numerous tall healthy trees.

As the coaches approached, a number of cottagers emerged from their homes to bob curtsies or make their bows, and as Sir Robert acknowledged them, he noted with satisfaction that all the buildings were in their usual state of good repair, with well-thatched roofs and neatly tended gardens.

He leaned back in his seat with a contented smile. The health and welfare of his tenants had always been one of his main concerns, and he was pleased to see that everyone appeared fit, and that the children all looked well fed, and active.

Aware suddenly of Mrs. Brace's eyes on him, he looked at her enquiringly but she averted her gaze towards Edgar, and asked him if he was all right.

'Yes, thank you, ma'am,' he replied with a shy smile, while Edward let out a whoop as Newsome's hunting horn announced they were approaching the gates leading to the estate drive. Hawton Hall, built by Sir Robert's ancestor Sir Oswald Masters in 1585, was not enclosed in trees and divided from the highway by a winding drive, like many of the country estates, but stood on raised ground at the end of a straight, broad pathway some quarter of a mile in length from the gate. There was no lodge, but half way along the drive to the right was the estate church and manse, while the stables, the smithy, and all other outdoor buildings were situated to the left.

It was to the rear and far right of the Hall, that the extensive and luxuriant grounds were laid, with countless orchards, tall trees, expansive lawns, a wide lake, and a large kitchen garden which also contained a number of hives. Like the village cottages, all the out-buildings including the church appeared to be well-structured, clean, and obviously recently painted; only the house itself looked somewhat shabby, and in need of attention.

Leaning out of the window, Sir Robert waved to Mick Harrant and his wife Juliet, the park gate-keepers, as they pushed open the low metal gates. They acknowledged his greeting before following the coach to where their cottage stood, at the side of the stables.

'There's a deer, Uncle,' Edward announced suddenly, jumping from his seat and pointing excitedly towards the Hawton herd which was grazing beneath some far trees.

'And there's some baby ones,' Lucy added, pushing her face up against the coach window.

'They're not babies, they're fawns, aren't they, Uncle?' Edward declared scornfully.

'Yes, they are, but be careful, Edward, you're pushing Edgar off his seat.'

Edgar's muffled reply was drowned by Mrs. Brace's voice, as she pointed towards the park.

'What very fine parkland you have, Sir Robert. And is that a lake I can see, on the far right?'

'Yes, indeed, my great-grandfather was a keen oarsman, and had the lake enlarged to its present size. It extends some distance across the park, and in parts is very deep. So the children know that they are not allowed near it without an adult,' he added, raising his voice.

'Yes, Uncle, we know, Uncle,' the twins chorused loudly, as Mrs. Brace then pointed to a herd of sheep grazing under the care of a young boy, some distance from the driveway. 'And that herd, Sir Robert,' she said. 'There are very few of them. Is this a new venture?'

'No, they belong to one of the villagers, Thomas Crumb. That will be his eldest son, Norris, tending them.'

'Then you did not enclose all your land?'

Somewhat taken aback by the keen gaze that was now directed at him, Sir Robert's reply was sharper than he intended.

'Not every landowner sympathised with the Agrarian Revolution, and the Masters family have always left part of their land accessible for the villagers to use.'

'I see,' Mrs. Brace replied, quietly. 'Forgive me, I did not mean to pry, I was merely interested.'

'Of course.' Embarrassed by his own reaction, Sir Robert tried to sound conciliatory. 'I quite understand, but sometimes we landowners are inclined to be improperly judged. The happiness and welfare of the tenants has always been of importance to my family, as you will no doubt observe, should you visit the village. And now, let us alight. We have arrived.'

Sir Robert gave a deep sigh as his eyes rested on what he considered to be his haven. Loving the house as he did, he failed to notice the scratched paintwork on the window frames; the ivy trailing uncontrolled up the walls; or the chipped stonework and the shabby entrance, at the top of a rather uneven set of stone steps.

He also failed to notice Mrs. Brace's look of disbelief as she stared up at the house. Neither did he observe her expression of distaste, as she examined the smoke which was belching in regular intervals from the fire in the hall. Nor did he notice how aghast she was, as she examined the chipped plaster mouldings on the walls, and the deeply rutted marble on the floor and wainscoting.

Delighted to be back in his beloved childhood home, Sir Robert was only aware of the customary happy welcome extended to him by Hawton's staff, headed by Harold Sinclair the steward, and Peterson the butler, who now both bowed deferentially to their master. Unlike his contemporary in London, Peterson was an approachable man with a pleasant disposition, and although firm with his staff, he had never been known to raise his voice and was always prepared to discuss a problem impartially.

'So very pleased to see you again, Sir Robert,' he now said. 'Everything is in good order, and we are all well.'

'Yes, indeed, so I see,' Sir Robert replied, happily. 'And Sinclair, how are the orchards and gardens? Has it been a good crop this season?'

'Indeed, Sir Robert, I think you will be well pleased, especially with the orchard.'

The two men continued to converse, and while Sir Robert enquired quietly as to the welfare and progress of his four young protégés whom, he had been gratified to see on arrival, looked particularly well, the twins played tag in between the servants. But Mrs. Brace continued to look askance at her surroundings. Remembering, suddenly, that he had omitted to present her to the staff, Sir Robert apologised profusely, and ushered her along the row of servants.

The introductions having been made, and Wenders and Hetty having arrived in the second coach, Mrs. Brace was escorted to her room, while Sir Robert handed the twins and Edgar over to Hetty's keeping.

Having had a number of other matters to discuss with both Peterson and Sinclair, two hours passed before Sir Robert climbed the stairs to his own apartment where Wenders had already laid out his master's evening clothes.

'I must have something done about that chimney,' Sir Robert remarked as he entered the room to be met by a smothered sneeze from his valet.

'I beg your pardon, Sir Robert, it's the smoke,' Wenders replied, but Sir Robert was now standing beside the window gazing with great contentment at the cultivated lawns and lake, which seemed to glow in the early twilight.

'I never feel so well as I do here, Wenders,' he said with a deep satisfied sigh. 'The house, the park, and the gardens, are all my Elysian fields.' He raised his arms and stretched luxuriously. 'Sometimes I think I should leave London and remain here for ever.'

'Do you, Sir Robert?' Wenders gave the smoking grate a jaundiced look, and shivered.

'Feeling the cold, Wenders?' Sir Robert looked concerned. 'It has been an unusually cool summer.'

'There is a draught, Sir Robert.'

'Yes, of course, that loose window. I must have it attended to. Sinclair has mentioned it more than once. But don't you find the air down here healthy and bracing?'

'Yes, Sir Robert,' Wenders agreed with a despondent sigh.

As Mrs. Brace had excused herself from dinner, apparently preferring to rest and eat in her room, Sir Robert ate a hearty meal alone in his cavernous draughty and smoky dining room. Waited on by two footmen, both of whom spent some time surreptitiously dabbing their watering eyes, Sir Robert sipped his excellent port, while contemplating how very good life had been to him.

Not only had he been blessed with loving parents and a happy childhood, he was also fortunate enough to be the master of a house considered to be one of the finest country dwellings in southern England. The loss of his brother and sister-in-law had grieved him deeply, but from that tragedy he had inherited two wonderful legacies on which to bestow the love he had lost, and for that, he would be ever grateful.

Awakening early next morning, Sir Robert dressed with the enthusiasm he always experienced in the country, and after descending the staircase and avoiding from years of habit the loose stair at the bottom, he hastened out to the stables, eager to take an early morning ride into the village.

Like all the surrounding domestic dwellings, the stables and all the other out-buildings were well constructed and cared for, and the animals were groomed and administered to impeccably. Two of the mares had given birth three weeks previous to Sir Robert's arrival, and he was eager to see the foals, both of which were female.

'They're in yonder stalls, Sir Robert,' announced Archer, the Head Groom, while the other stable hands nodded deferentially towards their employer. 'And young master's already there. Quite excited he is too.'

'Young Master Edward?' Sir Robert replied in surprise. 'Is Mrs. Brace here as well?'

'Mrs. Brace?' Archer shook his head. 'You be meaning the new lady governess? No, Sir Robert, it be young Master Edgar, not Edward who's here, and he came on his own.'

As if in response to Archer's words, a child's laughter suddenly echoed softly around the yards and Archer's young son Thomas appeared, followed by Edgar leading a small foal by a piece of rope around its neck. On seeing Sir Robert, both boys stopped but while Thomas acknowledged his master with a smile and a nod, Edgar's happy expression changed, and he stared up at Sir Robert in obvious apprehension. Concerned to see such fear on a child's face, Sir Robert smiled down at the boy.

'So, Edgar, you've discovered the stables and you're taking Scarlet's foal for a walk,' he said jovially. 'And what does her mama think of that?'

'Scarlet didn't seem to mind, sir,' Edgar replied hesitantly. 'Because it's Bluebird's foal.'

Obviously puzzled by the general laughter, Edgar continued to stare up anxiously at Sir Robert.

'Have I done wrong?'

'Of course not.' Sir Robert gave the boy a gentle tap on the shoulder. 'But I think we'll take her back to Bluebird now, and you can choose a horse to accompany me to the village. We have two ponies you can choose from. You'd like to do that, wouldn't you?'

Expecting his invitation to be acknowledged with enthusiasm, Sir Robert was disconcerted to see it had the opposite effect, because Edgar now looked even more concerned.

'I'm sorry, sir,' he muttered. 'But I can't ride. I never have.'

Sir Robert stared in surprise. George Randall was famous for his equestrian abilities at the hunt, and Sir Robert could not imagine why he had never attempted to teach his son the same skills.

'I see,' he now said, somewhat at a loss. 'And your Papa has never shown you how to ride?'

'No, sir, Mama wouldn't let him. She said it was too dangerous.'

'Ah, well,' Sir Robert smiled. 'I'll tell you what we can do. I shall ride Monty, he's a big horse, easily able to take two of us, and you will ride in front. You'll be perfectly safe. I won't let you fall.'

Whatever Sir Robert's stable staff thought of the sight of their master, trotting out of the yard holding a small boy tightly in front of his saddle, no one passed any comments at the time, but there were some light-hearted remarks later that night in the local inn, as to what 'Maister' might do next.

But the experiment proved a great success. Obviously delighted to be on a horse, and secure in the knowledge that there was no danger of falling, Edgar relaxed enough to respond to all the greetings addressed to him during the ride. Sir Robert was also able to discover with tentative questioning various details about the Randalls' home life.

'Mama's not been very well since Papa did the other things,' Edgar replied in answer to one of Sir Robert's questions.

'Indeed, how very sad, and how do these other things make her ill?'

'Papa is away so much at his work, and always returns looking strange.'

This was the second time Edgar had referred to his father's work, and Sir Robert tried to imagine what, to a nine year old child, would constitute *looking strange*.

'What do you mean *looking strange*?'

'He's always so muddy and dusty.'

Sir Robert frowned. He could visualize his friend with a haggard expression after hours at the card table, or even with some wine stains on his garments after trying to drink with an unsteady hand, but *muddy and dusty*? What on earth, he wondered, did George Randall do to achieve such an appearance?

By this time they had already traversed the village, and acknowledged a number of bows and nods, and were now trotting back across the park to the Hall. The previously sunny sky had clouded over, and rain had begun falling, so

Sir Robert spurred Monty to a gallop and they were just entering the stable yard when he felt Edgar stiffen slightly.

'Oh dear,' he said. 'There's Mrs. Brace, and she looks very cross.'

Sir Robert frowned. There indeed was Mrs. Brace, but she did not look cross, she looked furious. Assuming the reason to be the fact that, without her permission, he had taken Edgar riding Sir Robert handed the boy down into Archer's waiting arms and, dismounted, intending to apologise.

But before he could say anything, Mrs. Brace was by his side, eyes flashing and obviously quivering with rage.

'I wish to speak with you, Sir Robert, on a *most urgent matter,*' she hissed.

Sir Robert nodded, and tried to look as contrite as possible.

'Yes, Mrs. Brace, I am aware that I did not ask your permission to take Edgar ...'

'This has nothing whatsoever to do with Edgar,' she snapped back. 'It's the roof!'

'The roof?' Sir Robert stared down at her in surprise.

'Yes,' she almost snarled. 'The roof – the rain is COMING THROUGH THE ROOF!'

'Ah, yes,' Sir Robert nodded in agreement. 'There are certain places ...'

'Through the roof in the children's bedroom, their school room and ...'

Aware suddenly of the glances being exchanged between the stable hands, Sir Robert raised a placating hand.

'Can we perhaps discuss this in my ...'

But Mrs. Brace was already charging towards the nearest entrance to the house followed by Edgar, for whom an argument between adults had no novelty. Which probably why, when Sir Robert had joined them both in the hall, the child looked up at Sir Robert with a wistful look.

'Shall I have to go home now?' he asked.

'Good gracious no,' declared Mrs Brace. 'Why on earth should you?'

'Because you're cross and ...'

'I am NOT cross with you,' she replied firmly. 'And I'm very glad you enjoyed your ride. You must do it again soon. Meanwhile, go up to my sitting-room where Hetty will help you change into dry clothes.'

Obviously relieved, Edgar gave both adults a beaming smile and trotted off towards the staircase.

'Shall we ...' Sir Robert indicated the nearest drawing-room, but Mrs. Brace had already opened the door and was inside beside the fireplace before Sir Robert had a chance to move.

She still looked extremely annoyed, but Sir Robert was relieved to see that her initial fury seemed to have abated slightly, and wondered whether an enquiry as to how her arm was healing might placate her, But then decided against it, as instinct told him it was certainly not her health that was troubling her at the present time.

'Now, what exactly is it ...' he began with a smile, but he might as well not have bothered, for all Mrs. Brace's fury appeared to return as she glared up at him.

'You are apparently unaware, Sir Robert, that roofs and ceilings were invented to keep water out, not let it in! Also, smoke is supposed to go UP the chimney not DOWN! And there is that staircase ...'

'The staircase ...' Sir Robert repeated, mystified.

'YES, the staircase – the last step is almost LETHAL. Twice I have nearly fallen, and it is only because I am agile and take notice, that I have not broken my leg.'

Sir Robert felt himself beginning to get heated.

'Now really, Mrs. Brace, I think that is an exaggeration ...'

'Exaggeration you call it? Really, sir, you should discard all feelings of sentiment for this building, and view your home for what it is. A ramshackle broken-down house which has been neglected almost to the point of decline. I cannot criticise any lack of cleanliness, for the house receives its due share of scrubbing, but whatever glory it once had, and from the drawings I have consulted it was once a fine, Elizabethan establishment, now, through lack of care and attention, has almost been reduced to ruin. Why, your goatherd's dwelling gives better warmth and security than Hawton; and as to your beautiful tapestries and hangings ... Years without cleansing by an expert have almost obliterated whatever symbols or stories they were intended to illustrate! The floors also require attention. The only habitable area in the house is in the kitchen. So most of your servants gather there to eat, because the chairs and tables are solid and will not collapse, and there is a stove to keep them warm. Which brings me to the cold. Have you not noticed the draughts? I know it is only early Autumn, but the weather during the past few weeks has been particularly chill, and because the wind blows through the cracks, your servants are forced to wear warm garments beneath their livery. For a house of this size, with its high ceilings, and tall windows, it is essential to have plenty of fires for comfort, but with such smoky chimneys the fires are more of a hazard than an advantage. And yet,' she added in a more controlled tone, 'your grounds are tended with such loving care, and your stables are amongst the finest I have ever seen.'

Utterly stunned by this tirade, Sir Robert remained motionless, as though sealed to the floor. When at last he replied, he felt he was confronting judge, advocate, and jury, combined.

'I agree,' he said slowly. 'The house has been neglected, but it was not a deliberate act. You see,' he tried to explain. 'For me this house has always retained the beauty I knew as a boy. Most of my childhood was spent here, and it has always been my haven from the vagaries of the outside world.' He flushed slightly. 'I suppose I have loved Hawton rather as one loves one's wife. The imperfections of time are never noticed when one truly loves, and to try and change anything is tantamount to betrayal.'

'But my dear Sir Robert,' Mrs. Brace's voice had become suddenly gentle. 'Mending the roof and having the chimneys swept is not changing the house, merely tending it. Even in the most devoted of marriages, the participants must wash occasionally in order to remain compatible.'

Taken aback by her change of manner, Sir Robert began to laugh, and immediately the tension vanished as Mrs. Brace lowered herself onto the nearest chair.

'Indeed they must,' Sir Robert chuckled. 'And I know I have neglected this dear place. You say you have seen plans of the house? How interesting; it is some years since I studied them. I presume, therefore, that you are well acquainted with all of its nooks and crannies to ...'

'Supervise the repairs with your consent, of course,' Mrs. Brace added hurriedly.

'Yes, and Sinclair will be invaluable as to cost. He is as conversant with my finances as I am, or even more so. Now, I usually partake of a warm beverage at this hour, would you care to join me? And your arm, I must apologise for not enquiring as to whether it is healing satisfactorily?'

'Thank you, Sir Robert, my arm is much improved, but please excuse me for not joining you at the moment. I have the children's lessons to supervise, and ...' She hesitated, before continuing, 'I was much concerned by Edgar's reaction to our altercation.'

'Yes,' Sir Robert shrugged. 'The result of an unhappy home, I fear. The Randalls were once a devoted couple, but during the last two years or so they have grown very much apart. Which is why I hope Edgar can remain here until at least late January, when I shall be returning to London.'

Perhaps it was because Sir Robert was so distracted by thoughts of Edgar, that he did not notice Mrs. Brace's sudden frown when he mentioned London.

'You plan to return to town in January?' she queried. 'I only ask because it is probable that I may have to return there, just for a few days, in six weeks or so. It is not positive, but possible. I will advise you as soon as I am aware of the situation, and it will only be, as I say, for a few days. As to Edgar's reaction, I am sure he has over-emphasised his parents' disagreements. Such things happen occasionally in all marriages, or so I have been told.'

Then, before Sir Robert had an opportunity to question her as to what made it so necessary for her to take such a journey, or why she assumed the Randalls' present marital situation was trivial, she had walked swiftly across the floor and left the room.

As the door closed, Sir Robert lowered himself rather shakily onto the nearest chair. Apart from being overwhelmed by Mrs. Brace's verbosity, he was astounded by her assertiveness. But although she had almost insulted him by referring to his house as ramshackle and broken down, he was realistic enough to accept that Hawton did need attention, even if, previously, he had been reluctant to admit it.

His reference to marriage and longevity had been a sincere reflection on life as experienced by his parents. Theirs had been a happy house, and their sons had grown up within in it, secure in the love of parents who wanted only the best for their sons' welfare.

Such a home had always seemed to be calm, and Sir Robert was not a man for whom altercations of any kind were pleasant. His parents had always settled their rare differences amicably, and he could never remember hearing a raised voice from either, certainly not in his presence. Even with his brother he could never remember disagreeing, but Graham had been such a happy individual almost from birth, that it had been a pleasure to be in his company.

At the thought of his brother, Sir Robert gave a tremulous sigh. The great gap left by his death seemed never to narrow, and for a moment he closed his eyes in an effort to dismiss the pain. Then he remembered how Graham, just before that tragic accident, had suggested a surveyor should examine Hawton.

'Just to bring it more into shape,' he had suggested.

Was that why I have never done anything about the problems, Sir Robert now thought to himself? Because Graham is no longer here to help me? But his children are, and this house will be theirs one day. The thought invigorated him as he glanced at the flames trying to force the reluctant smoke upwards, without success. The sight reminded him of Mrs. Brace's outburst, and he grinned. I bet she tackles the chimneys first, he thought. She seems particularly provoked by the chimneys.

5

Within a week of Mrs. Brace's outburst, hoards of men with ladders, great wooden cranes and numerous roof tiles, took up positions outside the house, while four extremely grubby, and uncouth-looking sweeps invaded the interior.

Perhaps Sir Robert would have accepted these intrusions without protest if it had not been for the little boys accompanying the sweeps. He was aware of what he considered the heinous practice of forcing small children up chimneys, but had never encountered it. But as soon as he saw the four small, under-nourished urchins cowering before their masters, Sir Robert was aroused to a fury he displayed rarely, and only when justified.

In a voice that echoed through the house, he stated his objections and demanded that the sweeps used brushes.

'No child is to be used as a utensil in my house,' he fumed, before storming back into his sitting-room. 'And if the men persist, dismiss them. We can clean the chimneys ourselves.'

'I knew this would happen,' Wenders muttered to Peterson, as Harold Sinclair stared after his master in consternation.

'But what are we to do?' the steward declared. 'There are twenty chimneys, and the sweeps say their brushes are not long enough.'

'That can't be helped,' Peterson replied. 'They'll just have to manage somehow, without the boys.'

But the sweeps were not accustomed to *managing*, and loudly declared their opposition to Sir Robert's orders, stating that if he objected to them using the boys they would have to purchase longer brushes and he would have to bear the cost.

'Then we better pay them, and have done with it,' Sinclair muttered. 'But how long will it take for them to get longer brushes?'

No one had any idea, so the steward went to discover the length of the delay while everyone else agreed in some trepidation: '*She*'s not going to like it.'

While all this was going on, Sir Robert was sitting in his study ruminating on the disparity between the sad little urchins, and Edward and Lucy, and how the poor waifs would have benefited at the Coram Hospital, when he heard a scuffle beneath his window. Patting a growling Challenger, he leaned over the sill and discovered the four ragged little boys he had been considering minutes before cowering in the bushes.

'What on earth are you doing down there?' he enquired softly. 'Why aren't you with the sweeps?'

'Because they want to beat us,' the eldest-looking boy replied. 'Because they think we asked you for help.'

'That's nonsense, you never did any such thing,' Sir Robert declared.

'We told 'em that, sir, but they didn't believe us, so they don't want us no more.'

For a few seconds Sir Robert's fury returned, then, with a great effort, he calmed down and pulling the bell rope, requested Sinclair's presence. .

'Those children outside, the sweeps' boys,' he said as his steward entered the room. 'They tell me their masters are going to abandon them. Please find out if this is true, and in the meantime take them into the kitchen and make sure they are fed.'

Having anticipated this reaction from his employer, Sinclair nodded reassuringly.

'Certainly, Sir Robert, but I can advise you now without enquiring, the sweeps do hold the children responsible for your instructions, and are talking about ridding themselves of them on the way back to London.'

'Dear heaven,' Sir Robert declared. 'To be abandoned without food or shelter, miles from the city, would amount to murder.' He hesitated for a moment, then shook his head. 'There's no alternative, Harold. We must help them. Find out how these men procured them, and if the sweeps insist on payment, give them whatever they ask.' He shook his head and stared contemplatively at the steward. 'Some time in the future, such practices will not be allowed to continue, but until then those of us who care will have to do what we can. Explain everything to Peterson and ...'

'And Mrs. Brace ...?' Sinclair stared questioningly.

'Oh God,' Sir Robert groaned. 'I'd forgotten Mrs. Brace.'

'Don't concern yourself, Sir Robert,' Sinclair said reassuringly. 'I'm sure she will take it all in her stride.'

And of course, she did.

On being informed that her charges had once again multiplied, and on discovering that they all required, not only food but washing and a suit of clothes, she soon had the kitchen range relit, regardless of the smoke; instructed the four footmen to set about scrubbing; and found enough of Edward's garments to cover those parts of the children's anatomy that could not, even decorously, be left exposed.

'Some of the clothes are a bit tight,' she told Charles Henderson, the head footman,. 'But they will just have to do, until I go into town.'

'Actually, ma'am,' he replied. 'I think my mother could help you there. My youngest brother Tommy's outgrown his clothes, so they might fit.'

'Excellent, can you go and collect them today?'

'Er ... yes, ma'am, that is if Mr. Peterson ...'

'Oh, don't worry about him,' Mrs. Brace waved a dismissive hand. 'I'll explain the situation, and he will understand.'

Needless to say, while the four boys' personal welfare was being administered to, their future security was being heatedly argued out between their masters and Harold Sinclair, supported by Walter Rodgers, the estate blacksmith.

A man of immense stature, with a girth and arms to match, Walter was always summoned whenever an *awkward* situation had to be resolved. It was not that he was expected to contribute anything physical to the argument, he was just required to stand beside Harold Sinclair and *look.*

As always happened, the *look* succeeded - where Harold Sinclair's well-bred voice and polite persuasive manner might have had difficulties - with the result that, two hours after Sir Robert's initial explosion of wrath, everything was settled and harmony once more reigned in Hawton Hall.

'It was quite expensive, Sir Robert,' Sinclair explained. 'I'm afraid we have had to pay three pounds for each boy.'

Sir Robert shook his head. 'Dear heaven, what are we coming to, that a human life can be bargained for like any other commodity? But I could not bear to think of those poor little lads being disposed of like unwanted rubbish. And the sweeps, what of them? Are they bringing in longer brushes or ...?'

'No, Sir Robert,' Sinclair interrupted hurriedly. 'We have sent for replacement sweeps, with strict instructions that no boys are to be used. So, unfortunately, the cleaning of the chimneys has been delayed by two days.'

'Well, they've been belching out smoke for so many years, another two days is neither here nor there. And, er, Mrs. Brace ...' Sir Robert added hesitantly, suddenly remembering that although the governess had apparently accepted the increase in her duties, he had not yet consulted her.

'Yes, Sir Robert,' Sinclair murmured. 'Mrs. Brace has asked if she could see you.'

'Yes, I rather thought she would.' He drummed his fingers on the chair arm in a light tattoo.

But his concerns, as to Mrs. Brace's reaction, were immediately dismissed by her expressions of admiration immediately she entered the room.

'Such a very magnanimous gesture, to extend your protection to those poor children,' she declared. 'I have tried to discover their origins, but the three youngest were obviously handed over as babies; but the eldest, Jack Fullerton, the only one who has a name, lived with his mother in Stepney village. But when she died, about a year ago, he was sold to Mr. Crump by a neighbour. He tried to escape, but on being captured was so badly beaten, he's never dared try again. His back is covered in weals.' She gasped suddenly, before lowering herself onto the nearest chair. 'Forgive me,' she muttered. 'I am not usually so weak, but the sight of that poor child's back ...'

Moved, on realising that for the first time he was witnessing her compassion, normally concealed behind Mrs. Brace's self-possessed exterior, Sir Robert experienced a sudden feeling of remorse that he had never really attempted to get to know her, and when he spoke, his voice was unusually gentle.

'Please, do not apologise, it is most distressing to see how some of our less fortunate are treated,' he said. 'I know not how it can be changed, without an immense new attitude in the outlook of our nation. But, until then, we can only try and help where we can. The boy, Jack ... is there anything that can be done for his back?'

'Mrs. Honniton has applied ointments, but I fear, even when the scars eventually heal, he will be marked for life,' Mrs. Brace replied, her voice still quavering slightly.

'Mrs. Honniton, you are referring to the housekeeper?' Sir Robert remarked in surprise. 'I understood, from the message I received before you joined us, that she was to be away at her sister's home in Kent until the end of October.'

Sir Robert frowned, as he reflected how events of which he knew nothing, seemed to be happening at a remarkable speed.

'Mr. Sinclair thought it would be advantageous to have some assistance, in view of all the work about to take place in the house,' Mrs. Brace replied, her voice having recovered its customary briskness. 'I understood you had been told.'

Before Sir Robert could reply, there was a sharp tap on the door, and the housekeeper herself entered, looking concerned.

'Oh, Sir Robert, I now understand you were not aware that I had returned. If I had realised, I would have come at once to let you know, but I understood that Mr. Peterson had told you, but he said he thought Mr. Sinclair had informed you, whereas Mr. Sinclair thought ...'

'Yes, yes,' Sir Robert interrupted hurriedly. 'It is of no matter. I am delighted to see you, Mrs. Honniton, but concerned that you have curtailed your absence, due to problems in the house. I am sure we could have overcome ...'

'Not at all, Sir Robert, I was more than happy to return. My sister is a dear soul, and I love her greatly, but she can go on; and I have taken the liberty of bringing with me one of her maids, whom she no longer requires, A good, clean, girl called Bridget Edgeley, whose sewing is excellent, whereas mine, I fear, due to my rheumatic fingers these days leaves much to be desired.'

And with this, Mrs. Honniton bobbed a brief curtsey, before departing hurriedly through the door.

Sir Robert and Mrs. Brace exchanged glances and then, simultaneously, they began to laugh. When she had recovered herself, the governess was the first to speak.

'I fear,' she said with a rueful expression, 'I have caused a great upheaval in this otherwise calm and peaceful home. Not only have you been invaded by scaffolders, chimneysweeps, and various other workmen, you have acquired four orphans, and no one advised you as to the whereabouts of your housekeeper. May I suggest that perhaps, in the circumstances, you would prefer to return to London until all at Hawton has returned to its customary tranquillity?'

'Not at all,' Sir Robert replied, still chuckling. 'I am too intrigued not to be present for the next disruption, which I have no doubt will descend upon us very soon. But what of these orphans, are they to be taught a trade? Or do you consider that they should ply themselves in some occupation here on the estate?'

'I have been considering the matter,' she replied. 'As they are so very young - Jack is only seven years old, and the others but five years each - I thought that they should be allowed two weeks to adjust to a more decorous life. They have rarely been addressed without an oath, and their diction, and command of the English language is meagre, to say the least. They also have much to learn of the most basic details of decorum. Only Jack is aware that eating with one's fingers is not customary, and only he understands the requirements of Master Cummings' device.'

Sir Robert stared in consternation, but from his past experience of deprived children, this revelation was not a surprise. The flushing water closets now installed in Hawton Hall had been introduced by Alexander Cummings himself, and their presence had been the talk of the neighbourhood for weeks. In fact, the late Lady Masters had become convinced that some guests only accepted her invitation in order to avail themselves of these new devices.

'Err, what have they done to them?' Sir Robert asked apprehensively, as he remembered a similar fiasco in the past, when the first four orphans were introduced to these wonders of the modern age.

'They were apparently seeking something to drink, and on finding the closet appeared to think the water it contained was for drinking.'

'Oh God.' Sir Robert leaned back in his chair with closed eyes, and forgetting for a moment whom he was with added: 'At least they didn't do that.'

'Who didn't?'

'Oh, some young folk who came to work on the estate, a long time ago,' he muttered, growing hot.

'No matter,' Mrs. Brace replied, giving him a sharp glance. 'All will be explained, and Master Edgar is proving an invaluable asset.' She stood up and moved towards the door. 'I think I can assure you, Sir Robert, that there will be no further disruptions about which you need concern yourself.'

The door closed behind her, and Sir Robert shook his head as, resignedly, he prepared himself for the next calamity.

6

However, whatever disaster Sir Robert anticipated might happen during the following weeks, it did not arise. After the initial upheaval Hawton settled down to a rather boring, if noisy and dusty, routine.

The new chimney sweeps arrived within a week complete with extended brushes, and left eight days later, having brushed twenty chimneys scrupulously clean. The carpenters mended the stairs and replaced cracked woodwork; the roof tilers replaced the tiles; the stonemasons renewed some stonework and filled in cracks; and a number of women arrived to work on the tapestries, which now lay spread across the ballroom floor.

Of all the artisans in his house, these women intrigued Sir Robert the most. But as he had decided it was more tactful not to interfere in any of the refurbishments, he had hesitated to enquire as to who they actually were and from where they came.

He knew he could easily have asked Mrs. Brace, but due to her increased responsibilities he had scarcely seen her since their conversation in his sitting-room; and on the one occasion he had accosted her in the hall, she had shaken her head and rushed past before he had a chance to speak.

However, all his thoughts of the tapestry women were soon dismissed by a letter from Lord Haversham, explaining that there had been another violation of a grave; this time in Hackney village. Shocked that such atrocities were continuing to occur, Sir Robert was placing the letter in his desk when there was a knock on his door and Mrs. Brace entered.

'I have had appalling news,' he declared. 'There has been yet another violation of a grave. I cannot understand how the Runners can be so ineffectual. Surely by this time they should have made some discovery as to who is committing this outrage?'

'Indeed, one would think so,' Mrs. Brace replied, looking serious. 'May I enquire when this offence took place?'

'Last week,' Sir Robert replied. 'You may read the letter from Lord Haversham. It contains nothing private.'

'It would certainly seem the Bow Street Runners are not as efficient as one would hope,' she said, returning the note with a somewhat distracted expression.

'So inefficient, one is almost led to assume their skills are being directed elsewhere,' Sir Robert declared.

'Elsewhere?' Mrs. Brace queried sharply. 'Why, Sir Robert, what leads you to such an opinion?'

Surprised by her abrupt manner, Sir Robert frowned.

'My opinion is based on their apparent lack of interest. Surely it must be something even more serious which causes the Runners to disregard such atrocities. If their supervisors applied the attention required, I am convinced these crimes would be quickly solved. It is at these times, that I almost wish I had sought office in some capacity,' he added.

'The law?'

'That or Parliament.'

'Why, Sir Robert, you are yet young. Surely such a path is still open to such an intelligent and cultivated man as yourself. Your concern for those in poverty and want demonstrates an interest in public welfare, sadly lacking in the majority of our fellows.' Then, as though suddenly embarrassed by her own impetuosity, she added, 'But I beg your pardon, I am being presumptuous; and now I must to Mrs. Honniton as she has been asking for me.'

Perplexed, he stared after her as the door closed. She really was the most unpredictable woman he had ever encountered. In a crisis, she exhibited the calm, reliable attitude of someone capable of coping with any kind of problem, while apparently concealing a completely different personality.

There was also another aspect of her character which he found puzzling. Occasionally, she appeared to be lost in a mental world of her own, and on the second occasion Sir Robert had enquired as to the state of her injury, she had dismissed the matter as if it had been mere trivia which no longer concerned her.

She was, he concluded, an enigmatic mixture of awareness and indifference; but her remarks as to his own abilities had irritated him. He suspected that despite his generosity towards the waifs, she considered him to be a typical sybarite; self-indulgent and utterly detached from the basic problems of the world.

He sighed, because he had to admit it was partly true. He *was* detached and rarely stirred himself to abandon his beloved books. Even the twins' arrival had been adapted to fit in with the style of his life; and yet, he reasoned to himself, I have helped people, especially children. No, he frowned, I have supplied money and patronage, but with the exception of the twins, affection and welfare have been administered by others. So that, he decided firmly, has to change. And he glanced about the room, as if seeking a way to commence practising his new resolution. But the workmen and children had already been taken care of by more capable hands than his, so he decided to practise with the tapestry women.

He was approaching the ballroom when Edgar and the twins, accompanied by four clean and tidy small boys and an obviously adoring Challenger, appeared at the end of the corridor.

'We've been to see the Hugginots, Uncle Robert,' Edward announced importantly.

'The what?' Sir Robert frowned.

'The Hugginots, Uncle, the Hugginots,' Edward repeated, in the same irritated tone he had repeated the word 'elethumps'.

'He means the Huguenots, Sir Robert,' Edgar explained in a whisper.

'That's what I said, Hugginots and they speak French,' Edward declared, looking cross.

'Of course, of course,' Sir Robert replied controlling a laugh. 'But where are you all going?'

'To see the horses,' Edgar explained. 'Mrs. Brace thought we ought to have some fresh air, and we thought we'd take Challenger. You don't mind do you, sir?'

'Not at all,' Sir Robert replied, stepping back to let the procession pass before continuing to the ballroom.

The lack of sound from within surprised him, but on opening the door he discovered everyone was too immersed in their work for chatter. Seven large tapestries lay spread across the floor, and kneeling before them working industriously were a number of women. Nervous of disturbing them, Sir Robert entered as quietly as possible but his efforts proved futile because immediately all the women rose to their feet and curtsied.

Remembering Edward's remarks about the women's language, Sir Robert greeted them in French, and then asked from where they originated. The women exchanged glances, before one of them explained in English.

'We are French emigrés, Monsieur, My name is De Vaul, and my daughter and I fled from Paris during the Terror, but my companions are Huguenots, and have lived in your country for over a century. We all reside in your area of Spittle Fields.'

As the woman was speaking, Sir Robert noticed that two of his protégés Patsy and Grace were assisting some of the women and seeing his glance, Madame De Vaul smiled.

'Master Sinclair requested that the girls might assist us as we work, as he tells us it would be to their advantage to learn to be seamstresses.'

'Indeed,' Sir Robert agreed. 'But I came to enquire whether there is any way I could be of assistance to you all during your stay?'

Madame De Vaul shook her head. 'Madame Honniton has made us most comfortable, Monsieur. It is a pleasure to be in your house.'

Later that day, still determined to become more involved in the lives of the children now in his care, Sir Robert was about to seek them out when there was a knock on his door, and Mrs. Brace entered.

'Forgive me, Sir Robert, but could you very kindly spare me a moment? A problem has arisen for which, if it is at all possible, I need your assistance.'

Intrigued to learn in what way he could possibly aid this more than capable and efficient woman, Sir Robert stared at her expectantly.

'It is the children, Sir Robert.' she explained hurriedly. 'You see, tomorrow the painters will arrive and pandemonium will reign.'

Sir Robert listened intrigued. If what he had suffered during the past two weeks was not pandemonium, he could not imagine what further chaos she had planned.

'The tilers are well away from harm, being on the roof,' she began. 'And, as I believe you already know, the carpenters are almost finished and the women working on the tapestries are secure in the ballroom. But the painters will invade initially all but those particular areas, and must have access to all other spaces and rooms. Despite this building being a large house, I am at a loss to know where to put the children, and Mrs. Honniton is most concerned regarding their welfare.'

'But surely they can be kept occupied somehow. I was only thinking earlier that you might arrange some academic ...'

'That is the problem, Sir Robert. I will not be here. You will no doubt remember that I said I would have to return to London for a very short visit. I will be away for only five days, and return next Friday.'

'But ...'

'So I thought,' she continued, hardly drawing breath, 'that you could perhaps employ them with some activities, such as riding, or fishing, or perhaps shooting. Edgar has expressed a wish to learn how to handle a gun. And I am sure boating would also be acceptable. All the children say how they would like to visit the lake; and you will not in any way be concerned with their domestic matters which will be cared for by Mrs. Honniton and Hetty.'

Sir Robert hesitated. It was all very well to make resolutions and then contemplate them mentally, but it was an entirely different situation having to accomplish them physically. He was also somewhat irritated that Mrs. Brace had *told* him of her forthcoming absence, rather than requested permission to take her leave. After all, he was her employer, and although she had done far more in the short time of her employment than her position warranted, she should remember that she was subservient to his commands.

But before he could remonstrate, she was already outside in the corridor and Sir Robert found himself addressing an empty room. Still provoked, he decided to tactfully obtain Wenders' opinion of his sister's behaviour.

'We are to lose Mrs. Brace tomorrow,' he said later that day, as his valet was assisting him into his evening coat.

'Yes, Sir Robert, I fear so,' Wenders replied in mournful tones. 'She has unavoidable matters to attend to in town.'

'I see,' Sir Robert said not at all mollified. 'And am I to assume that these unavoidable matters relate to the ventures to which you referred?'

'Er, it is a possibility, Sir Robert, but my sister does not confide in me, so I fear I cannot assist you. Will you be requiring anything further, Sir Robert, before dinner?'

Realising that there was no point in continuing the conversation, Sir Robert thanked the valet rather tartly and dismissed him.

As Mrs. Brace had departed before Sir Robert arose, he was unable to pursue the matter of her behaviour further, and anyway such thoughts were soon dismissed when he found himself surrounded by seven small children, all of whom assured him that they had been told by Mrs. Brace: 'Sir Robert will look after you while I'm away.'

Just what that assurance involved he now realised, as he comprehended the complications of keeping a group of active and animated children occupied, for anything up to nine hours a day.

Then he noticed that a small piece of paper had been pinned to each of the waifs' jackets. Bending down to get a closer look, he saw that the two nearest notes read *Matthew,* and *Mark,* while on the third jacket was written the name *Timothy.*

'Why ...' he began, only to be quickly interrupted by Jack.

'It's Mrs. Brace's idea, Sir Robert. When she found they hadn't got names, she said if they all had Disciples' names it would give them a good start. But they kept forgetting who they were, so she pinned on their names. I didn't need one because I know who I am.'

Nothing Sir Robert had experienced during his travels through London's grimy streets evoked a more powerful picture of degradation, than Jack's innocent explanation with regard to the three waifs' names. Possibly created unwillingly they had been discarded at birth like unwanted parcels, and would have fared better had they been whelps or kittens, since no doubt *they* would have then been given names and cared for until they could fend for themselves.

Sir Robert closed his eyes for a moment, as though to dispel the mental vision that seemed to persist in his mind. He suddenly became aware of a certain amount of shuffling, and glancing down found seven small faces gazing intently up at him.

'Are you all right, Uncle?' Lucy asked him with a worried look.

'Yes, yes, sweetheart, of course I am,' Sir Robert assured her hurriedly, as he tried to drag his mind back to the present. Then, looking down somewhat helplessly at his charges he said, 'Er ... what shall we do?'

'Perhaps we could learn to ride, Sir Robert' Edgar murmured. 'You said you would teach me, and I know the others would like that as well.'

'Oh, yes,' echoed six trebles. 'We would.'

'Thank you, Edgar, that is a very good idea.' Sir Robert tried not to sound relieved. 'We better go to the stables and see what Archer can suggest by way of mounts.'

What the painters, industriously wielding their brushes, the tilers suspended on their cradles, and gardeners and indoor staff thought of the crocodile of children marching determinedly after their urbane leader, was concisely expressed by one of the visiting joiners who muttered to himself as they passed, 'He be a right one, he be!'

Archer, having been consulted, produced two plump little Welsh ponies, a hunter well past his jumping days, and Scarlet, the Cleveland Bay mare, whose foal still lived with her.

'They're all as quiet as lambs, Sir Robert,' Archer said reassuringly. 'Only thing is Scarlet won't move unless little Penny goes along as well. But she's no trouble, does everything her Mama tells her.'

'Really,' Sir Robert replied, somewhat unconvinced. 'Rodgers told me she could be difficult. Perhaps we ought to take Bluebird? She doesn't mind leaving Fancy behind.'

'Afraid she's not herself today, Sir Robert. Nothing serious, but her leg's a bit swollen; and Penny'll be like a lamb, Sir Robert, so long as she's close to her dam. And anyways, Thomas'll be going along with you, so he'll keep her quiet.'

As he followed his troupe of would-be equestrians and their mounts out of the stable yard Sir Robert noticed the two pigeons perched on the stable roof. Ordinarily, he would not have commented, but unlike their companions their feathers were not a mottled mixture of white, grey, and black, but an abundant and brilliant white.

'Where did those two come from?' he asked, indicating the two birds. 'They're not part of any flock around here.'

'Sorry, Sir Robert,' Archer replied with an apologetic shrug. 'I'm afraid I've no idea. They just appeared one morning. But they come and go.'

'Come and go,' Sir Robert echoed. 'What on earth do you mean?'

But Archer was already some way ahead, so Sir Robert gave the birds one last glance, before concentrating on his new responsibilities.

The following two hours, Sir Robert admitted later, were the most enjoyable he had spent in years. Having removed his jacket, and clad only in shirt, pantaloons and boots, he demonstrated how to both mount and dismount; how to hold the reins; and how to urge the animal with gentle stabbings of heels against its ribs.

As none of the children had ever mounted a horse before, they all approached the situation according to their personalities. Both Edgar and Jack, between whom a friendship had been formed, quickly negotiated the complexities of initial horsemanship; while Mark, and Timothy, being more hesitant, clung nervously to their saddles. But to Sir Robert's surprise it was Edward, Lucy, and Matthew, who exhibited true prowess, and were soon trotting confidently across the open field.

Delighted by his small relatives' equestrian abilities, and anxious to encourage the others, Sir Robert would have enjoyed another hour's teaching, but the sight of Archer approaching, reminded him that it must be nearly time for whatever meal children ate at mid-day, so he told his charges, with some reluctance, that they had to return to the house.

Disappointment was obvious as crestfallen little faces turn pleadingly towards him, and Sir Robert nearly hesitated, but then he remembered the absent governess.

'I am afraid we must stop because Mrs. Brace would have wanted us to.'

The alacrity which this announcement produced was astonishing; and all seven children were soon obediently following Archer, Thomas, and the horses, back to the house and the ministrations of Hetty and Mrs Honniton.

Leaning contentedly on the gate as they marched away, Sir Robert recalled those times when, as a boy, he had accompanied his father and brother around the estate to examine the different trees and study the various wild plants and flowers which abounded during the summer months.

Such wanderings at the moment were still possible, as there would be plenty of fallen leaves and vegetation to study. Even if the weather was getting cooler, the children could still learn a great deal which could not be achieved within the confines of the schoolroom.

Feeling satisfied with his first attempt at trying to be a part of the 'real world', Sir Robert gave himself a theoretical pat on the back and picking up his coat, flung it jauntily over his shoulder before striding contentedly back to the house.

7

Despite enjoying the involvement with his new charges, Sir Robert found Mrs. Brace's absence strangely unsettling. It was not as if he had seen her regularly - she had been too preoccupied - but it was the knowledge that if he had required her presence she would have been there to respond, and this, he now realised, had been reassuring.

The expression: 'Perhaps you should consult Mrs. Brace,' was now everyone's response whenever a problem arose, especially with regard to Sir Robert. Which was why he particularly missed her voice which, except for its one hysterical outburst, had always seemed melodic and in control. Her absence also made him aware that apart from the female servants, she was the first woman to inhabit the house since his mother's death.

Occasional female visitors from neighbouring estates had been invited to Hawton, but their visits had also included an escort of either husband, or brother. Mrs. Brace's position in his house was of a more intimate nature, a circumstance he had not fully appreciated until now, and one which he found strangely disturbing.

However, she had left him with an important task, and realising that on her return she would probably request a report on the children's progress Sir Robert decided it was necessary for him to become fully acquainted with each of the boys as individuals.

Although he had formed attachments to them all, he found himself drawn particularly to Jack; possibly because the boy had been more aware of his previous life.

A quiet but articulate lad, his few months with his tyrannical master had scarred him mentally, as well as physically, and possibly because of this Sir Robert at first found the boy wary, and obviously nervous. But gentle and persuasive words soon succeeded in drawing out all Jack could remember of a childhood which, until his mother's death, had been affectionate and secure.

The appalling act which followed this tragedy was perpetrated by one Mick Taylor, a neighbour of Jack's mother in Stepney, and the act of selling Jack to Master Crump had taken place the night after her death.

'He just came and dragged me away,' Jack muttered. 'He said we were going to see the Vicar, but we didn't, and I don't know what happened to my mother.'

The implications behind this revelation made Sir Robert shudder inwardly. How long had the poor woman lain unburied? Or had her body been cast pitilessly into unconsecrated ground or even the river, without any form of religious rite to which even the most humble were entitled?

The more Sir Robert dwelt on Jack's story, the colder his fury became until he vowed that, no matter the difficulties involved, he would avenge the child's wrongs and bring Mick Taylor to justice. His thoughts must have registered themselves in his expression, because suddenly Jack drew back, obviously nervous.

'I didn't do anything,' he began to whimper. 'Because I couldn't.'

Immediately, Sir Robert leaned down and gathered the child into his arms.

'No, no,' he said. 'I am not angry with you, but with ...' He hesitated not wishing to arouse sad memories again. 'Life, I suppose,' he finished lamely.

They were sitting on a wooden bench beside the lake watching the other children trying to collect tadpoles. It was now the sixth day of Mrs. Brace's absence, and Sir Robert had become so accustomed to his guardianship position the world of fashion far away in London had lost all relevance.

Now, with Jack leaning against him and the other children laughing excitedly, and calling to each other, Sir Robert relaxed against the tree trunk and smiled to himself, until Jack's voice interrupted the silence.

'What did you mean, sir, about life?'

'I was reflecting on how life can be kind to some people, and very cruel to others,' Sir Robert explained.

'Like me having a bad life, and you having a good one?'

Taken aback by the child's discernment, Sir Robert stared down in surprise.

'Yes, I suppose I do. But your life is not going to be bad anymore. It's going to be full of good things and kind people,' he added, quickly.

'But it'll never be like yours, sir, because we were born different,' Jack insisted.

'Our parents may have come from different places, which meant that we followed different lives, but everyone can change, Jack. You will have that chance and so will your friends, because you will be educated and taught how to care for yourselves; and when you are old enough you will learn a trade, or some occupation that will help you earn your living.'

Before the boy could answer, Edgar came running up shouting that they had caught a frog.

'It's in the net,' he yelled. 'We don't know what to do with it.'

'You must free it at once,' Sir Robert declared, rising up. 'Come, show me quickly now before it gets injured.'

For the next few minutes seven pairs of anxious eyes watched, as Sir Robert tried to tempt the frog to jump out of the net. At first the creature cowered and refused. Then suddenly, it seemed to gather itself together, and with one leap landed safely in the lake.

There was a united cry of 'Hurrah,' after which Sir Robert returned to his seat beneath the tree. Perhaps it was because he felt so at ease that after a few minutes his fell asleep, and there is no knowing how long he would have remained unconscious, if he had not been awakened by a woman's voice, gently calling his name.

Opening his eyes he discovered Mrs Brace, surrounded by the children, smiling down at him.

'Uncle Robert's been asleep,' Lucy announced, as Sir Robert scrambled hurriedly to his feet feeling particularly flushed.

'Yes,' Edward agreed. 'And we might have drowned.'

'You haven't been ...' Sir Robert began aghast.

'Of course they haven't been in the lake,' Mrs. Brace replied briskly. 'Edward is being dramatic, and that's very foolish of you, Edward,' she added sharply.

'Sorry,' Edward replied with a crestfallen expression.

About to reassure his nephew that nothing was wrong, Sir Robert hesitated. Then, bowing to a more knowledgeable authority, listened as Mrs. Brace continued her admonition.

'It's not a good idea to frighten people, Edward, and I'm sure you won't do it again.'

Edward shook his head vigorously, and Mrs. Brace gave a satisfied nod.

'Now,' she said, 'I'm sure you are all hungry, so we will return to the classroom for your tea, and the first one there gets an extra cake.'

There was a general dash for the house, as Mrs. Brace waited for Sir Robert to collect the discarded fishing nets with an enthusiasm he could not quite understand. As he did so, he gave her a surreptitious glance. She appeared to have lost a considerable amount of weight, because her previous rather dumpy outline had acquired contours, and her figure was considerably shapelier than before her departure for London.

Perhaps, Sir Robert reasoned to himself, it's her clothes. They were certainly more fashionable than the garments she had worn in town, and he wondered if her hasty departure had been taken to replenish her wardrobe. But that was such a frivolous reason to take six days leave, and one thing Sir Robert had learned about his governess was that she certainly did not indulge in frivolity.

All his original irritation at her abrupt behaviour had been long forgotten and reluctant to appear inquisitive, he enquired as nonchalantly as possible whether she had accomplished all the tasks which had called her to town.

'Yes, thank you,' she replied smiling. 'But I may have to return when you do in January. By that time, the children will be confident enough of their new life to bid us farewell and continue living at Hawtom. I am referring of course to the four boys, not Edgar and the twins.'

Sir Robert frowned. 'Would it inconvenience you to have the other four boys in London?'

'No, but ...' Mrs. Brace's voice trailed off, and she stared at him in obvious surprise. 'Is it your intention then that they should all return to Grosvenor Square? Would not the healthy surroundings of Hawton be more beneficial?'

'Possibly, but I would like to see them develop with education and guidance. During your absence I talked to them all quite intimately, and they are all malleable and intelligent, and respond well to gentle persuasion.' Suddenly aware that Mrs. Brace was studying him closely, Sir Robert frowned. 'As you are probably already aware, I have on occasion tried to aid such folk to the best of my ability. Now, I suggest we return to the house; those clouds are heavy so it is bound to rain very soon.'

Feeling suddenly embarrassed, he did not wait for her response but commenced striding towards the house, very aware of Mrs. Brace following close behind.

That evening, after Sir Robert had retired to his bedroom to read, there was a knock on his door, and to his surprise Edgar entered in his night-clothes.

'Why, lad, cannot you sleep?' Sir Robert declared rising from his seat.

'Yes, sir, but before I do I would like to speak with you.'

'Come in, and sit beside me,' Sir Robert indicated the chair nearest to the fireplace. 'Now, what is troubling you?'

'I would like to take Jack home with me,' Edgar began, hesitantly. 'But I do not think Mama and Papa would be very pleased. I wondered if you could speak to them, and explain that we are friends now. I like him very much, and it is the first time I have had a real friend.'

Almost breathless after possibly the longest sentence of his young life, Edgar sank down onto the proffered chair and stared up anxiously at Sir Robert, who stared back in equal concern. He was more than able to give refuge and support to destitute youngsters because, as a bachelor without anyone to object, he was able to do as he pleased. But whether George and Madeleine Randall would share his opinions, he very much doubted.

'Have you mentioned this to Jack?' He asked at last, and was relieved when Edgar shook his head.

'No, sir, I thought I would ask you first.'

'Well, Edgar, perhaps you could let me think about this for a while. I cannot promise anything at present, not until I have spoken with your father and mother.'

'But you will try,' Edgar said pleadingly.

'Yes, I will try,' Sir Robert replied, hoping he did not sound as unconvincing as he felt.

Later, Edgar having returned to his room, Sir Robert sought out Mrs. Brace, who received the news with raised eyebrows.

'It was bound to happen,' she said. 'Living in close proximity with a child who, if nature had planned differently, would probably have been as capable as Edgar of growing into a gentleman.'

'Most probably, but nature did not plan it that way. So what am I going to do?'

'Really, Sir Robert, I can only suggest that you write to Lord Randall and explain.'

'But what about Lady Randall?'

'Oh, she will not mind, I am sure.'

This was said with such confidence that Sir Robert frowned.

'You appear to be very aware of Lady Randall's proclivities. Do you know her?'

To his surprise, Mrs. Brace flushed suddenly and it was a few moments before she replied.

'When it was arranged that Edgar would accompany us to the country, I called on Lady Randall to enquire as to any special needs he might have. She expressed her delight that he was to be included, and explained he had no particular likes or dislikes. Now, Sir Robert,' she enquired abruptly. 'What of my suggestion, do you think it would be propitious to write to Lord Randall?'

'In view of the fact that Lady Randall is so delighted that Edgar is with us, something I was not actually aware of until now, I think she would be more inclined to agree with regard to Jack.'

'Possibly, as to the other children, have you observed that their speech is becoming more intelligible? In fact, I suspect they are attempting to adjust to the twins' and Edgar's vowels,' she added with a laugh. 'But now, Sir Robert, you must excuse me. I have brought some winter garments with me from town for the smaller boys, and there are one or two adjustments I have to make to those Mrs. Henderson has given me.'

With which words Mrs. Brace opened the door and, as was her custom, disappeared into the corridor.

8

Sir Robert's quandary, on how to word a letter to Lady Randall regarding Edgar's request, seemed to increase with every hour, until, in some desperation, he again approached Mrs. Brace.

She was seated in the window-seat of her sitting-room, stitching a boy's pair of pantaloons, as Sir Robert entered.

'Mrs. Henderson was an exemplary seamstress,' she said. 'These garments were so well sewn, they will last the children for some time.'

'Indeed,' Sir Robert replied. 'That is most providential, but I would be grateful for your advice yet again on Edgar's request. I am aware that Lady Randall should be approached, as you suggested, rather than her husband, but as to exactly how I should word such a letter I am somewhat at a loss. You see ...' he struggled.

Mrs. Brace gave him a sympathetic glance.

'Would it be of assistance if I were to write to Lady Randall myself?'

Relieved, but reluctant to burden her yet again he sank down into the nearest chair and gave her a rueful grin.

'It would indeed, but I do not like to inflict yet another problem on you. Considering you were employed only as a governess to the twins, you have been over-burdened to a quite disgraceful degree.'

'Not at all, Sir Robert,' she replied. 'After all, writing such a domestic letter is more the province of a woman rather than a man.'

'Well, I am grateful nevertheless,' Sir Robert insisted. Then, to his annoyance, felt himself flush under her steady gaze.

The next day, somewhat to his surprise, he received a letter from a military acquaintance,

Major Lord Stransbury, from whom he had not heard for over two years, the major having been stationed in Paris since Napoleon's banishment to St. Helena. Curious as to the reason for this sudden correspondence, since their friendship had not been a close one, Sir Robert broke the seal and was perplexed to discover that after the usual preliminaries as to his good health and welfare, Lord Stransbury wished to know whether Sir Robert was acquainted with any of the individuals guarding the ex-Emperor on St. Helena; and was he aware of the name Balcombe.

Sir Robert's first reaction was to dismiss the question as nonsense, but good manners reminded him that such behaviour was not the way to react to correspondence from someone he respected and had always considered a friend, if a rather distant one.

So he opened his desk and replied that he was not, and had never been, aware of anyone associated with the island of St. Helena, and had never before heard of the name Balcombe. Then in order to soften the asperity of his reply he enquired after the major's family, and hoped they were all well and enjoying their sojourn in Paris.

Having despatched his reply down to the post, Sir Robert dismissed the matter from his mind, and realising Lord Stransbury had probably not intended his words for anyone but the recipient, locked the letter away in his desk.

As early winter began to spread itself across the countryside, and red berries sprouted from many of the bushes surrounding the house, an almost a daily procession of workmen drove their great carts away down Hawton's drive.

If some of them glanced back with satisfaction at the house as they departed, they were entitled to. The tall, elegant Elizabethan building with its restored roof, cleansed flint and stone dressings and new paintwork, now seemed to glow with pride as it must have done when first erected in 1580.

The last to leave were the seamstresses, with whom all the children had become very friendly. To the extent that both Jack and Edgar had acquired enough French to be comprehensible, while the other five could all manage basic greetings and short phrases. So it was a sad little group that stood waving dejectedly to the elegant brougham, with which Sir Robert had replaced their original wooden wagon, as it departed briskly down the drive.

'Will we ever see them again?' Matthew asked dolefully, his little face screwed up to try and prevent tears.

'Of course,' Mrs. Brace reassured him, with a gentle hug. 'There is always some needlework to be performed, so I am sure Sir Robert will have use for them again in the future.'

'Certainly,' Sir Robert agreed. Then, hoping to cause a diversion, he continued, 'And now, as we have the ballroom free, I thought you might all like to commence your fencing lessons.'

There was a general yell of agreement, but as the children immediately scampered back into the house Mrs. Brace shook her head.

'Their exuberance is understandable,' she said. 'But do you have foils small enough for their use?'

'Indeed, yes,' Sir Robert replied, trying not to sound complacent. 'For when you mentioned the possibility of them learning to fence, I arranged for a short piste to be laid out on the ballroom floor, and ordered a number of foils of the correct size, to be sent over from an armoury in Portsmouth, together with suitable canvas jackets, and wire masks.'

'How very resourceful of you, Sir Robert, and you do not have to concern yourself with regard to me either, for I have my own épée.'

'You have an épée? ' Sir Robert stared at her in surprise, as it was more customary for a woman to use a blunted point foil, rather than a duelling sword.

'Yes, I was given lessons when quite young, in order to correct a bad posture,' Mrs. Brace replied briefly.

'I find it hard to imagine you ever suffered from such a problem,' Sir Robert said, glancing at her straight back and dignified carriage. 'But I would still question the advisability of you performing with an épée. Surely a foil is more appropriate?'

'Because I am a woman, I suppose? Surely, Sir Robert, with your modern outlook and admiration for Mary Wollstonecraft, you would not criticise my support for women?'

Surprised by her apparent knowledge of his opinions, and also the sudden light-hearted manner in which she addressed him, Sir Robert hesitated for a few moments before replying.

'My remarks were intended neither as a criticism of your abilities, nor did they in any way refer to the excellent Mrs. Wollstonecraft, but were merely a comment on the advisability of a woman sparring with an épée.'

'Then you have nothing to fear on my behalf, for I am fully conversant with the weapon and aware of its dangers.'

Her voice had acquired a firmness which brooked no argument, so there was nothing further discussed except that they would meet in the ballroom later that day, to give the children their first lesson.

When he was once again alone, Sir Robert crossed to the window and stood for some time gazing out at the park, while trying to imagine how Mrs. Brace had become so conversant with his political views. So far as he was aware, none of his staff in London, including Wenders, knew anything. While at Hawton, only Harold Sinclair was aware of that side of his master's life, and nothing would have persuaded him to divulge any secrets.

Sir Robert was still ruminating on the subject when, having changed into his heavy canvas jacket and collected his wire mask and gloves, he entered the ballroom where all seven children and Mrs. Brace awaited him, similarly dressed.

The lesson commenced with Sir Robert and Mrs. Brace demonstrating how opponents saluted each other with their foils, and then in slow movements, how each opponent had to attempt to touch his adversary.

'It's the lightest of touches,' Sir Robert explained. 'You are performing a sport, not fighting a foe.'

Fascinated the children watched until, assured that they had learned enough to attempt the sport themselves, Sir Robert handed out the foils and the children paired up with Mrs. Brace opposing Lucy.

At first, they all responded with more enthusiasm than skill, but within half an hour to Sir Robert's surprise, it was obvious that Timothy, Matthew and Mark, showed considerable promise, whereas the remaining boys and Lucy seemed reluctant and hesitant in their strokes.

After a further ten minutes, as all the children were beginning to tire Mrs.Brace suggested that they had a rest, and perhaps try again the following day.

Everyone agreed, but as Sir Robert was about to remove his mask Edgar turned to Mrs. Brace, and murmured something in her ear.

'I have no idea, Edgar, you will have to ask him. I am quite agreeable if he is.'

'Ask me what?' Sir Robert said.

'That we should have a bout together. I am quite happy to play, but I would prefer my épée rather than a foil.'

Somewhat taken aback, Sir Robert frowned. 'I have no objection but are you quite sure?'

'Perfectly,' Mrs. Brace replied briskly.

So it was that, watched by seven pairs of fascinated eyes, Sir Robert found himself having to prove that he was as good as his female opponent. An opponent, he was somewhat disconcerted to discover, whose fencing dexterity was far in advance of his own. In fact, Mrs. Brace's parries and ripostes seemed so relentless that, at last, Sir Robert had to admit defeat, and to the accompaniment of the children's applause, lower his épée.

'Indeed, madam, your teacher must have been exemplary, but you also have a natural aptitude for the sport,' he said, ruefully.

'Thank you, Sir Robert, but I must return the compliment,' Mrs. Brace replied, with a smile. 'The way you parried my thrusts was quite masterly. I have not encountered such a move before.'

'You play regularly?' Sir Robert asked in surprise.

'Only when the opportunity presents itself,' Mrs. Brace replied somewhat sharply. 'Now children, collect your weapons and place them on that chair, together with your masks and gloves, and we will go down to your room for tea.'

There was a general bustle as the children obeyed, and the ballroom quickly reverted to its customary state of subdued elegance.

Pulling off his gloves and canvas jacket, Sir Robert looked down at the collection of foils now resting on the chair. Yet again, Mrs. Brace had revealed another surprising accomplishment. Was there anything the woman could not do? And where had she learned such skill with the épée? Or, more interestingly he thought, from whom had she learned such a skill? There was, of course, only one way to discover how she had acquired such prowess, and to discover the identity of her teacher.

But Sir Robert never had an opportunity to broach the subject, for within an hour of her departure from the ballroom she entered his study looking concerned.

'Sir Robert, I must beg your indulgence yet again, for I fear I have to return to London as soon as possible, within the hour in fact. The matters of which I spoke, and which I understood had been settled, have not been resolved. I will be away but a few days, but you need have no concerns regarding the children, as Hetty has been helping me teach the four boys to read, and write. I have also asked Mrs. Honniton to kindly assist Hetty with regard to the changing of clothes, and other domestic matters. I am most distressed to disturb your life yet again in this way; Sir Robert, but I do have some good news,' she added, before he had a chance to reply. 'Lady Randall has agreed to take Jack, which will delight Edgar, and be of immeasurable support to him. Now, with your leave, I must depart.'

Then, without waiting for Sir Robert's reply, she turned and whisked out of the room. He sat down heavily on the nearest chair. The woman was quite impossible. What, in heaven's name, was so urgent that she had to leave for

London almost without warning? And why was she not more explicit? Women, and certainly governesses, did not tear about the country on the slightest whim; it was undignified and improper.

He sighed heavily. Of course he would not be inconvenienced, as the children were now occupied with schoolroom studies, and this time she had not made any suggestion as to his own involvement. But he would participate: there was bound to be some form of instruction in which he could be of use. Somewhat cheered by this thought, he arose and was about to pull the bell rope for a footman, when he heard the sound of horses hooves receding from the house. Frowning, he hurried to the window and was astonished to see two mounted figures galloping through the entrance gate towards the village.

That one of the riders was Mrs. Brace he had no doubt, although she appeared to be clad in male attire and was riding astride like a man; before he could summon a footman to discover what was going on Wenders entered, looking harassed.

'My apologies, Sir Robert, but my sister asked me to tell you that she has taken one of the hunters, Admiral I believe, and she ...'

'In Heaven's name, man,' Sir Robert exclaimed, 'why didn't she take a carriage?'

'Begging your pardon, Sir Robert, but she did not care to encroach further on your benevolence.'

'Benevolence, what's benevolence got to do with it? She's got a two day journey before her, and who is her companion? And what happens if they meet some footpads, or even a highwayman?'

'Her companion is Thomas Archer, a most reliable young man,' Wenders replied hurriedly. Then, seeing this news had in no way diminished Sir Robert's displeasure, he shook his head. 'I fear my sister has always been headstrong. But I can assure you, Sir Robert, she is well able to take care of herself.'

'She'll certainly have plenty of opportunity,' Sir Robert replied, grimly. 'So far as I am aware, young Thomas has only his fists with which to defend himself. So let's hope she's taken her épée with her, or I'll be seeking the abilities of another governess before winter ends.'

'Yes, Sir Robert,' Wenders agreed meekly and then, obviously deciding retreat was the wisest course, he departed hurriedly from the room.

Later that evening, having first resolved to confront Mrs. Brace on her return to demand an explanation for her extraordinary behaviour, Sir Robert attempted to restore some form of order into his life by reading a few pages of Homer's *Iliad,* but without success. His mind kept returning to the eccentric sight of his governess, clad in man's attire, pounding her way down the drive towards the highway. However, one pleasant distraction which had helped to restore Sir Robert's customary equanimity was Edgar's joy when he learned that his parents had agreed that Jack could become his companion.

'For ever and ever,' Edgar had gasped, his hands tightly clasped together.

'Certainly until you are old enough to go to school,' Sir Robert explained. 'When you go to Eton, Jack may have to stay behind to learn a trade or profession.'

'But will Papa and Mama pay for that?' Edgar asked, looking concerned.

'I shouldn't worry about that now,' Sir Robert said reassuringly. 'I am sure they will do something but, remember, I shall be around to help, if help is needed.'

If Edgar was ecstatic, Jack's reaction disturbed everyone; because on being told the good news he stood stiff and still while tears ran profusely down his cheeks. It took a great many cuddles from Hetty, and reassurances from Sir Robert, to restore the child's usual humour on learning that his life, from now on would be one free of fear and abuse.

Reflecting on the scene later, it only intensified Sir Robert's determination to hunt down Mick Taylor and make him pay for his crimes. For some reason, this reflection reminded Sir Robert of his communication from Lord Stransbury, and going over to his desk he unlocked it. But on pulling open the small drawer he stared down in shocked surprise; the letter was no longer there. The drawer was empty.

9

For a few moments Sir Robert stared down at the empty drawer in disbelief. No one apart from himself had a key to his desk; and as he had always carried the key on his person how had the drawer been opened?

Then he remembered that during the fencing bout the previous day he had become rather heated, and removing his canvas jacket had placed it on a nearby chair. As none of the children had been near the chair during the entire morning, the only person who could have removed the key would have been Mrs. Brace.

He was still standing transfixed, trying to quell the realisation that, not for the first time, events were evolving over which he had no control, when there was a knock on the door and Wenders entered. The unfortunate man could not have appeared at a more inopportune moment, for the sight of his valet reminded Sir Robert of Wenders' close relationship to Mrs. Brace and he turned angrily on his employee.

'Enough is enough - who and what is your sister? I demand to know. Someone has been pilfering my private drawer and a letter has been removed. There is only one key, which I have always retained on my person. Someone stole it, and I have reason to believe it was her. She is not just a governess, is she?'

The last words were declared with such venom the valet recoiled slightly, and his agitated reply was almost a whisper.

'I only know she is working in some way with our government, Sir Robert. And that the recent desecration of graves is involved. I begged her to explain her situation to you, but she said any explanation would reveal the identity of other people, whose lives might then be endangered. I know only that some part of it has to do with the ex-emperor.'

'Napoleon?' Sir Robert exclaimed.

'So I believe, Sir Robert.'

'And is that the reason she left so abruptly?'

'I would assume so.'

'What do you mean *assume so*? Don't you know?' Sir Robert demanded.

'I fear she has not confided in me, Sir Robert,' Wenders' reply was almost inarticulate. 'I know only that she was called away urgently, and I came to advise you that Thomas Archer has now returned, with Admiral.'

His anger abating slowly, Sir Robert stared perplexedly at his valet.

'Returned? But how on earth has she continued her journey?'

'Apparently she alighted on the high road, and Thomas hailed the Stage. If you please, Sir Robert.' Obviously, almost overcome, Wenders lowered himself slowly down onto the nearest chair.

'Why on earth, oh, never mind, and for goodness sake man, pull yourself together. You say she had been called away. How could that have happened? No strangers have visited the house, and there has been no post apart from my letter since last Monday.'

Wenders stared miserably back at his employer. 'She is in the habit of using an air transport procedure.'

'Good Lord! Is that where those two pigeons came from?'

Apparently by now devoid of speech, Wenders nodded.

The absurdity of the situation suddenly hit Sir Robert, and controlling a wild desire to laugh he looked sympathetically at his unhappy valet.

'And does she use this air transport procedure in London?'

'Yes, Sir Robert, she has a coop on top of a nearby house which she visits at night.'

'At night?' By now, Sir Robert was too intrigued to be anything other than curious.

'Yes, when we are all sleeping she goes across the roof tops and collects her messages.'

'Goes across the rooftops!'

'Yes, Sir Robert, she has always been remarkably agile.'

'Good God! Is that how she got her injury the night I was at the opera? What happened, did she fall off the roof?'

'Er, not exactly, Sir Robert, she was attacked.'

'Merciful heaven! Who by?'

'I fear I am unable to tell you, Sir Robert, because she refused to disclose his name.'

'And I suppose you have no knowledge as to how she is involved with the desecration of graves, or why she indulges in literature concerning cadavers? And presumably all these activities commenced some years after you joined my household, so were never known to my mother when she recommended you to me?'

His face a picture of misery, the unhappy valet shook his head.

'Well, this is all very mysterious, Wenders.' Sir Robert stared reflectively at the unfortunate man. 'And I am sure you will agree most unsatisfactory. Although I do not hold you responsible for your sister's ... What did you call them? *Ventures*? ... I do think you should have given me some indication when you recommended her, that she had a private and somewhat unorthodox life apart from that of being a governess. She was, after all, in sole charge of two beings whose lives I hold dearer than my own.'

Wenders nodded dejectedly. 'I am aware of my failings, Sir Robert, and fully appreciate the reason you will be dismissing me.'

'Dismissing you?' Sir Robert exclaimed appalled at such an idea. 'I've no intention of dismissing you. You've been with me twelve years, man. I couldn't possibly manage without you.'

Obviously relieved by his employer's outburst, Wenders arose on unsteady legs and gave a slight bow.

'Thank you, Sir Robert, and I apologise for my silence, but my sister has always been headstrong, and although she is much younger than me she has always been very domineering.' He sighed, heavily. 'You see, she is the daughter of my father's second wife, my own mother dying soon after my birth. And Harriet, for that is her name, was and is a kind and gentle lady, who has always treated me as she would have done her own son. Even after Amanda was born she continued to bestow on me the same concern and affection. But I fear she has been perhaps too liberal, especially with Amanda, who has always been allowed great licence to do as she pleases.'

Anxious to learn more about Mrs. Brace, and how she had become involved in what appeared to be a political conspiracy, Sir Robert leaned forward encouragingly.

'And this is how she became a participant in this particular venture?'

'I fear it would appear so, Sir Robert,' Wenders replied with a sigh. 'Although all I know is that she sends and receives messages. She has never divulged anything else of a serious nature, apart from her unfortunate accident. For some weeks last year she was in Paris, but again I have no knowledge of why she was there, or for what reason. I did not see her on her return as she went directly to stay with a friend of our late father's, Captain Maitland.'

'Maitland? Do you mean the Captain Maitland of the *Bellerophon,* to whom Napoleon surrendered?'

'I believe so, 'though I have never met the gentleman myself. Will there be anything further, Sir Robert?'

'Er, no thank you,' Sir Robert replied. Then a sudden thought occurred to him. 'And did all these activities commence when she became a widow? Or was Mr. Brace an active participant?'

As if attempting to remove a constriction in his throat, Wenders drew a deep breath.

'I fear there never was a Mr. Brace, Sir Robert. My sister has never been married. She decided to call herself a widow, as she believed this was more respectable while working in a house devoid of other female company, apart from Hetty. Again, I must submit my most abject apologies for deceiving you. I fear my sister has a very strong manner, and ...'

'Yes, yes, man, I have already gathered that,' Sir Robert declared, subduing an unexpected feeling of elation. 'I accept your apology, but did you have no qualms that you were involving me in her schemes?'

'Oh, yes, Sir Robert,' Wenders almost wailed. 'But there was no question of schemes at the beginning. Amanda genuinely required an income, as Harriet is unable to support her; and I thought she would be of assistance. It was only after she joined your household that I discovered the extent of her activities. When I did, I tried to persuade her to give notice but she refused because she said the twins needed her. She has become extremely fond of them,' he finished lamely.

'And they of her,' Sir Robert replied dryly. 'And that is my greatest concern, their welfare and their disappointment at her absence. For this reason, am I to assume she does intend to return? Or do you recommend I seek the services of another governess?'

'If I may call upon your great depths of tolerance, Sir Robert,' Wenders gasped with a stricken expression, 'I can assure you my sister has every intention of returning, and will no doubt communicate with you soon.'

'Very well,' Sir Robert replied. 'And I assume that what has been discussed just now should be regarded as a private matter between the two of us.'

'Oh, most certainly, Sir Robert,' Wenders declared, obviously shocked at the idea that anyone else might become involved.

'There is one other matter,' Sir Robert said, reflectively. 'Her fencing prowess, where did she become so accomplished?'

'Our father was considered an expert and attempted to teach us both. I am afraid my achievements were miserable, but Amanda displayed an ability that surprised everyone.'

'I can quite understand that,' Sir Robert replied tersely.

As soon as Wenders had departed, Sir |Robert stood staring reflectively at his desk while still trying to assess how Mrs. Brace had managed to purloin his key unnoticed, and then return it without his knowledge..

He was still deep in thought, when there was a sharp knock on the door, and Edgar and Jack entered.

'Please, Sir Robert,' Edgar began. 'Could we go outside now? We've all done our lessons for this morning, and Mrs. Honniton says there's another hour before lunch.'

Dragged back from mysterious happenings to the more demanding tasks of the day, Sir Robert was soon distracted by his pupils' equestrian efforts and his own pleasure at their achievements. It was as he was leading everyone back to the stables that Lucy catapulted him back to the complexities of the morning.

'When will Mrs. Brace be coming back?'

Sir Robert frowned. Reluctant to say he had no idea, he replied briefly that she would probably be back the following week.

'Where's she gone?' Edward looked up at his uncle enquiringly. 'And why did she go?' he added, almost as an afterthought.

Feeling helpless, Sir Robert was glancing around as if seeking assistance when Jack came unexpectedly to his aid.

'Don't you know it's rude to ask questions?'

'Sorry,' Edward muttered looking crestfallen.

'It's all right,' Sir Robert reassured him hurriedly. 'She's gone to London to see someone about ... a puppy.'

'For us!' Seven voices yelled in unison.

'Er ... yes,' Sir Robert replied, feeling vanquished.

'But Thomas told us that Susie's had three puppies. We could have one of those,' Lucy declared.

'No, this must be a special puppy,' Edward announced importantly. 'Susie's puppies are ordinary.'

'No, they're not,' Matthew protested. 'They're lovely.'

'Yes, they are,' Timothy and Mark agreed loudly.

'All right, all right,' Sir Robert yelled above the din. 'Susie's puppies are promised to other people, that's why Mrs. Brace has gone to get you all a special one.'

Later that afternoon as the children were being supervised by Hetty, Sir Robert tried to decide what to do about the problem that was Mrs. Brace.

Although he tried to regard her behaviour as outrageous and tantamount to a betrayal of his trust, the vision of her clad in men's clothes, not to mention her agility at fencing, kept intervening, as did the brilliance of her eyes and the clear smoothness of her complexion. He frowned as he attempted to remember that she was also a bossy self-opinionated woman, who had had the effrontery to disrupt his household by her antics. But despite these reassurances, he had also to admit that he admired her courage and determination to carry out whatever endeavours she had been assigned to do. She was also compassionate and understanding, or she would not have accepted the four waifs and administered to them with such sympathy.

Confused by feelings he considered illogical, considering the situation in which he had been placed, Sir Robert decided to try and subdue them by dealing with the urgent matter of the children's education. Despite Wenders' confidence that Mrs. Brace intended returning within the week, Sir Robert did not regard this as a guarantee and therefore some action had to be decided on immediately.

Although Mrs. Brace had assured him that Hetty was capable of helping with elementary grammar and mathematics for the six younger children, Sir Robert realised such tuition was insufficient for Edgar. He had been given into Sir Robert's care on the understanding that he would receive the same treatment he was used to at home, and this included an intermediary education to prepare him for public school.

There was also another responsibility that Sir Robert had to consider. It was now only four weeks away from the 6th

December, when according to Hawton tradition the Christmas festivities commenced. Followed three weeks later on the 25th December, with a gathering of all Hawton's tenants and staff to enjoy a feast of food and drink.

But it all had to be supervised. Sir Robert tapped his fingers irritably on the windowpane. All this continuous ruminating was not getting him anywhere; immediate action was what was needed. He summoned Harold Sinclair to explain that as usual the customary Christmas festivities would be taking place.

Sinclair looked delighted. 'We were wondering, Sir Robert. With Mrs. Brace leaving like she did, we thought you might be spending the festival in London.'

'No, I would never do that,' Sir Robert reassured him. 'And with the weather getting much colder, we must be sure that there are plenty of logs for all the fires.'

Then Sir Robert noticed the first snowflakes beginning to flutter gently down towards the driveway. At once his problems seemed to recede slightly. If it got really cold, the lake might freeze over and he could teach the children to skate; and there would be snowmen to build, and snowball fights as well. With luck, these distractions might dismiss all thoughts of Mrs Brace from the children's minds, even if they did not dismiss her from his.

10

Three days after her departure a letter was received from the erstwhile governess, addressed to Sir Robert, and marked *Strictly Private*. It explained that she would have to be away longer than she had originally planned, due to the unexpected illness of a close relative, but hoped to be returning to Hawton by 6th December. Sir Robert showed the note to Wenders, who shook his head despondently.

'We don't have any other relations apart from Harriet, and she lives in Edinburgh now with one of her cousins. I've no idea what my sister is talking about; and of course there is no address.'

'I had noticed that,' Sir Robert replied dryly. 'But I suppose we must be grateful she didn't send it by Pigeon Post, and I also note that she doesn't mention the stolen letter.'

Wenders' face seemed to wrinkle slightly. 'Are you sure you would not prefer me to leave?' he muttered.

'Of course not,' Sir Robert declared briskly. 'As I said before, we have to face this together. So plans must be made for the continuance of the children's education. Especially Edgar's, as his parents are under the impression that it is being supervised by Mrs. Brace.' An idea suddenly occurred to him. 'I have no objection to trying to teach him some Latin, but ...' He hesitated, before adding, 'To what standard were you educated, Wenders?'

'Me, Sir Robert?' The valet stared in surprise. 'Why, I attended a good Dame school when small, and then was privately educated at an Oxford academy until I was seventeen. I would have continued, if my father had not died and I had to commence supporting my step-mother and sister.'

'So you're conversant with subjects like history and geography?' Sir Robert asked enthusiastically.

'Er, yes, Sir Robert, to a certain degree,' Wenders replied, looking doubtful.

'Splendid, then you can teach Master Edgar those, while I cover Latin and some mathematics.'

'Teach, Sir Robert?' Wenders' eyes widened to their extremity. 'You wish me to teach?'

'It's not difficult,' Sir Robert replied, encouragingly. 'He must have some grounding in the subjects already. After all, he is nine years old, and I remember vaguely Lord Randall mentioning something about a tutor during one of our conversations. And, of course, he would also have been studying the subjects with your sister, when she deigned to honour us with her presence,' he added laconically.

Wenders winced. 'Er ... yes Sir Robert, but ...'

'So all we have to do is discover which period in history he was covering,' Sir Robert continued, ignoring the interruption. And as for geography,' he added, waving his arm explanatorily. 'It's just a case of him studying the globe.'

'I think there's a little more to it than that, Sir Robert, if I may be so bold as to say so,' Wenders murmured. 'There are the different localities in each of the continents, and ...'

'Yes, yes,' Sir Robert declared impatiently. 'But we have to try. Now, let us go up to the schoolroom and investigate what facilities are available.'

Whatever Sir Robert anticipated he might find, he did not expect to see the five younger children concentrating avidly on a blackboard, on which Albert was industriously writing letters.

As the two men entered all the children immediately stood up, and the young page bowed.

'We're doing handwriting, Sir Robert,' he explained. 'Mrs. Brace left instructions that handwriting should be done in the mornings and reading in the afternoons.'

'I see,' Sir Robert replied, somewhat at a loss. Then realising Edgar was missing, asked where he was.

'Mrs. Brace said that as he was more advanced, she has left him some sinonums and antonums for Hetty to teach him.'

'What on earth are those?' Sir Robert declared.

'I think he is referring to synonyms, and antonyms, Sir Robert,' Wenders's explained, his eyes twice their normal size. 'Is it possible that Hetty is teaching Master Edgar English grammar, Sir Robert?'

Sir Robert stared at the page in astonishment. 'I was not aware that my nursery maid was so erudite. When, pray, did she learn and where is this phenomenon taking place?'

'She learned it at home, Sir Robert,' Albert explained. 'She can read and write beautifully, and they're in Mrs. Brace's parlour because it's nice and quiet. Jack's with them because Mrs. Brace thought he should learn these things as well; and until she returns she said I was to do this,' he added.

'If I may venture to say, Sir Robert,' Wenders murmured softly, 'it would appear my sister has taken care to cover all eventualities with regard to the children's education. Although, of course,' he added hurriedly, 'it might be advantageous to discover the extent of Hetty's knowledge of English grammar.'

The scene in Mrs. Brace's parlour reminded Sir Robert of his own early studies, when he and Graham had sat carefully copying out words under the supervision of their mother.

Seated at two small desks, with Challenger stretched out on the floor, and Hetty perched on another chair with an open English primer in front of her, Edgar and Jack were writing down words at her dictation.

As the two men entered the boys stood up and Hetty curtsied.

'If you please, Sir Robert ...' she began.

Wenders, unable to control his curiosity, interrupted. 'Where did you learn about English grammar, Hetty?'

'Millie Newsome, if you please, Master Wenders.'

'Millie Newsome,' Wenders repeated, while Sir Robert stared in astonishment.

'Yes, sir, Master Newsome taught her because he believes in women being educated, begging your pardon,

Sir Robert. And when I said I would like to learn as well he taught me the alphabet rhyme. The *A was an apple pie, B bit it, C cut it, D dealt it, E eats it ...*'

'Yes, yes, Hetty,' Sir Robert declared, interrupting hurriedly. 'I am aware of the poem and it is a very commendable way to learn the alphabet. But we will delve no further,' he added as Wenders attempted to speak. 'And just accept that I appear to have a remarkably erudite staff, who apparently spend their leisure hours pursuing the heights of knowledge.' Then in a gentler tone he said with a smile, 'Am I to assume that Mrs. Brace discovered all these attributes, and assigned you the task of deputy governess?'

'She asked if I could help, Sir Robert,' Hetty replied with another curtsey, 'and she left me this book. It explains where words come from and is especially for children. I haven't done nothing wrong have I, Sir Robert?' she asked nervously

'On the contrary,' Sir Robert enthused. 'I am delighted at your prowess, but I think we should divide the various aspects of Edgar's education between us until, of course, Mrs. Brace's return. You continue to teach him whatever English grammar Mrs. Brace has left for you to do, and I will occupy the hour before lunch to assist him with his Latin.'

'I am not very good at Latin, Sir Robert,' Edgar declared looking concerned. 'Mr. Meadows told me I had no opitude for Latin.'

'You mean aptitude,' Sir Robert replied briskly. 'And I was not very good at it either. No one ever is – so don't worry, we will approach it very slowly.'

For the next two weeks Hawton Hall became, to quote Sir Robert, a veritable hive of learning. Three hours every morning were devoted to academia, while the afternoon was spent either indoors perfecting their fencing skills, or outdoors exhibiting their riding abilities.

It was probably because he was so absorbed by the novelty of his new life that Sir Robert did not concentrate on the passing of time. So it was with some surprise that one morning, two weeks before Christmas, he glanced through his study window to see a large yule log being conveyed by cart up the driveway. Simultaneously there was a knock on the door and Harold Sinclair entered.

'Morning, Sir Robert,' he said. 'It won't be long now, sir. Shall I arrange for the usual hog roast?'

For a second, Sir Robert stared in mystification at his steward then reality dawned.

'Good heavens! Of course, it's nearly the 6th December. I hadn't realised. Yes, of course you must arrange everything as usual, and I must make sure that all the villagers and everyone else hereabouts is aware that we will be holding the usual gathering on the 25th, after church.'

'With respect, Sir Robert ... Mrs. Brace said.'

'MRS. BRACE!' Sir Robert's response seemed to bounce noisily off the walls.

'Er yes, Sir Robert.' Sinclair's eyes suddenly appeared twice their normal size. 'She ... she returned last night and ...'

'No matter,' Sir Robert replied, fighting for self-control. 'Order the hog roast and all the other things we have. Where did you say Mrs. Brace was?'

' Er ... I didn't, Sir Robert, but I believe she is resting.' Then without waiting for a response, the hapless steward almost fled from the room.

It took some time for Sir Robert to regain his composure. That the infernal woman had returned without notifying him was bad enough, but she had the audacity despite having a houseful of responsibility to be *resting*. He began to pace the room until, at last, having exhausted himself, he sank onto the nearest chair and tried to decide what to do.

For nearly an hour Sir Robert fumed, ruminating on one course of action and then another. Then at last he realised that despite the many folk with whom he was surrounded, and the many acquaintances he had, there was no one in whom he could truly confide or turn to for advice.

Most men of his age were married, and if the unions were happy ones they had someone to share their problems and of course their joys. Sir Robert gave a rueful grin. Perhaps he should have spent time cultivating a companion, and not persuaded himself to believe, just because of one failure, that most women were fickle creatures unworthy of his love.

Perhaps that was his problem. He had judged all women to be as worthless as the first. Yet, although he had always supported his mother's view, that all women should be permitted the same educational advantages as men, the past still permeated his thoughts. As though that one mistake so long ago, would inevitably repeat itself should he ever pledge his heart to another.

He sighed heavily. He knew he was being foolish to think in this manner. It had occurred over thirteen years ago, when he had been young and vulnerable, without any experience of women, which was why he had been so easily duped.

But all this introspection did not solve the problem of Mrs. Brace. Only she was not Mrs. Brace, after all. She was very much Miss Brace, or Wenders, or whatever else she called herself. He glared ominously around the room, all his prejudices returning. That woman was no better than ...

At that moment there was a sharp tap on the door, and the governess herself walked into the room.

11

For a few moments they stood staring at each other. Then motivated by a sensation he had never before experienced, Sir Robert strode across the room and taking Mrs. Brace firmly in his arms, kissed her passionately. As her response was equally passionate they remained embracing each other until, shaking slightly, Sir Robert released her.

'Forgive me,' he muttered incoherently. 'I ...'

But before he could continue there was a knock on the door, and Peterson entered.

'My apologies, Sir Robert,' he said, 'but Mrs. Brace is required in the nursery, as an emergency has occurred.'

'Of course,' Sir Robert replied in a somewhat strangled voice, as Mrs. Brace walked calmly from the room.

Alone, he sank into the nearest chair. What on earth had come over him? To behave in such a way towards a woman who was dependent on him for her living was beneath contempt. But she had not repulsed him. In fact, he was astonished to admit to himself that she had apparently welcomed his embrace, and had certainly not looked in the least disconcerted when she left the room.

Could she possibly have feelings for him? His own for her were almost too complex for him to consider. One minute he thought her an interfering over-bearing woman, and the next ... He sighed. It had been so long since he had held a woman that he had forgotten how delightful the sensation could be; and their moment of passion had awakened emotions which he had believed long dead. She had felt so perfect in his arms; warm, soft, and responsive.

He struggled out of his chair, and poured himself a brandy. The clear light brown liquid glowed in the firelight, and that, combined with the now gathering dusk, restored Sir Robert to a semblance of calm as he tried to decide on his future behaviour towards his governess. He could not just ignore what had happened. So an apology was necessary, and perhaps a written one would lessen the embarrassment of the situation.

For a while, he pondered as to the wording, and then finally decided a straightforward apology without too much explanation would be the best. But when it was finally written, after more than four attempts, he sat staring at it disconsolately.

Dear Mrs Brace, Please forgive me for taking such a liberty. I can assure you it will not occur again. I hope, therefore, that you will be kind enough to accept this apology, which is most sincerely given.

What was he going to do, if she was so insulted she relinquished her post? With all those children in the house, such an action would be a catastrophe. Then a sharp knock on the door made him start and he rose nervously to his feet, but it was only a footman to light the candles so Sir Robert sank back onto his chair in relief.

Two hours later, his note having been given to a servant to deliver, Sir Robert retired to the library where, after ordering his dinner, he remained undisturbed until Wenders entered, to enquire as to when he wished to retire.

'Er ... in about an hour, I think,' Sir Robert replied with a cautious glance at his valet's face. 'Are all the children in bed?'

'Yes, Sir Robert, and have been for the past four hours. In fact, everyone has retired sir, except for yourself.'

As Wenders did not appear, or sound, like a furious brother determined to avenge the insult to his sister, Sir Robert took some consolation from his valet's apparent ignorance of his faux pas and retired thankfully to bed.

The following morning, while other staff members bustled about hanging holly, ivy, and other evergreens, Peterson entered to explain that Mrs. Brace was taking breakfast in the nursery, due to a *slight mishap* the previous day. Remembering some reference to the *urgent matter* which had caused her to depart so swiftly after their union, Sir Robert stared enquiringly.

'Young Mark, Sir Robert, he climbed a curtain, but I'm afraid the curtain could not bear his weight and it fell down with him underneath. Got a nasty knock on his head, but Mrs. Brace says there's nothing broken. But he's a bit upset, so she's staying with him in the nursery.'

'I see. Er ... why was he climbing the curtain?'

'A bird, Sir Robert, it flew in through an open window and he wanted to catch it so that he could let it fly away.

But, as it happened, his efforts were needless because after flying round the room the bird simply flew out of the window.'

Sir Robert sighed. 'And the curtain?'

'Mrs Brace is arranging for it to be rectified at this very moment,' Peterson said reassuringly.

Having completed his breakfast, Sir Robert tried to decide whether Mrs. Brace's lack of response to his note was indicative of her outrage, or simply a superior form of nonchalance at his behaviour. If it were the latter, it might indicate that he was not the first man to force his attentions on her, and she had accepted them as a natural phenomenon; but this he very much doubted. Which meant that his most tactful approach to the problem would be to absent himself from the house long enough for her, hopefully, to realise that he was truly penitent.

So for the remainder of the morning Sir Robert rode Monty across his estate, visiting the farms and cottages. But for the first time, the sight of his tenants and their obvious pleasure at his visit, did not give him his customary enjoyable satisfaction. At last, feeling very downcast and having reached the church entrance he dismounted, and after tying up Monty entered the building.

Quite what he had hoped to gain, Sir Robert was not sure; but the familiarity of a building he had known all his life and where both he and his brother had been christened and confirmed, seemed to envelope him in an invisible, but ensuring, mental cloak. His family pew seemed to welcome him like an old friend, and as he sank down onto his customary seat it was as if all his earlier trepidations and concerns were slowly sliding away.

How long he sat just absorbing the atmosphere he had no idea, until the creaking church door indicated someone was entering. For a moment, apprehensive that it might be Mrs. Brace he jumped to his feet, but it was the Vicar's son Nicholas Carter, who walked through the doorway carrying a number of books.

'Oh, Sir Robert,' he declared. 'Forgive me, I did not intend to disturb you.'

'Not at all,' Sir Robert replied.. 'I just came in for a while and will be leaving shortly; and it is I who intrude.'

Nicholas shook his head. 'No, Sir Robert, to enter God's house is never an intrusion. The door is always open to all. As I am sure you are already aware,' he added, as if realising suddenly to whom he was speaking.

Sir Robert nodded, and then sat watching as Nicholas stacked his books carefully onto a shelf before commencing to dust the pews. As the only child of the incumbent vicar, he had been expected to follow his father's profession, but Nicholas, although a dutiful son in other ways, had declared his wish to study the law and was due to commence at a Cambridge college the following September.

He had almost completed his dusting when Sir Robert remembered that there had been rumours of a romance between Nicholas and the daughter of a vicar in the next parish. Not wishing to appear inquisitive but curious as to whether the rumour was true, Sir Robert turned to where Nicholas was now standing.

'So you are to leave us in September,' he said. 'And before then, have you any other plans?'

Nicholas flushed, but when he spoke his voice was clear and concise.

'I am not sure what you have heard of my friendship with Grace Kell, Sir Robert, but folk have placed more importance on that friendship than it deserves. We are both too young. I am not yet nineteen, she two years younger, and I wish to establish myself afore so important a step.' He looked hesitantly at Sir Robert, and then flushed again. 'You see, I believe that a man has a certain feeling when he meets the woman to be his wife. My Mama told me that when she met my father, she just knew. She couldn't explain it, she just said I would understand when it happened to me, and it hasn't happened with Grace. Begging your pardon, Sir Robert, I hope you will forgive the liberty.'

'Of course, I consider myself privileged to be the recipient of such a private matter,' Sir Robert murmured. 'You have sound sense, and deserve to succeed. I will no doubt see you many times before you leave, but please accept my good wishes now for your future, and the achievement of your ambitions.'

Apparently too overcome to reply, Nicholas gave a swift bow and hurried out of the church. Once more alone, Sir Robert wandered down to the altar and after making obeisance, left the church and mounted his horse. He was not quite sure what had happened to him during his time in church, but one thing he did realise was that the 'certain feeling' so determinedly described by Mrs. Carter to her son, was exactly the same emotion he now felt for Mrs. Brace.

133

12

On arriving back home Sir Robert was not surprised to be told that Mrs. Brace wished to see him, whenever convenient.

'Something to do with gifts I understand, Sir Robert,' Harold Sinclair explained. 'She wants your agreement as to cost.'

'Cost? Surely you can agree whatever sum she wishes to spend,' Sir Robert replied rather stiffly.

'Er …yes, I suppose so, Sir Robert, but she was very firm in her request.'

'Oh, well, you had better tell her I am free, but give me a few moments to read this.' He waved a piece of hand-written paper at the steward who, after nodding in apparent understanding, left the room.

Sir Robert stared down at the innocuous list of farm horses being offered for sale; the words could have been written in Chinese for all the impact they made on the reader.

Should he apologise again? Or should he wait to see her reaction, before saying anything? Alternatively, should he behave as if nothing unusual had happened? But that could be construed as either cowardice or impertinence, emotions which he abhorred. So instead he pulled the bell rope, and with a nonchalance he was far from feeling told the footman that he awaited Mrs. Brace, at entirely her own convenience.

The following fifteen minutes were, up to that particular point in his life, the longest Sir Robert had ever experienced, and when her heard her brisk footsteps approaching along the corridor, he had to take a deep breath in an attempt to appear composed. But whatever feelings she may have been harbouring with regard to his embrace, they were certainly not apparent when she entered the room and closed the door.

'The curtain has now been mended,' she began.

'The curtain?'

'Yes, Sir Robert, the one that Mark climbed. It was not a serious tear and has been very well sewn, but to digress from domestic matters Sir Robert, we should talk.'

'Er…yes,' Sir Robert replied, trying to make his voice sound as matter of fact as his companion's. 'But I would like to confess that …'

'That it is not your custom to envelope females in such a manner as occurred yesterday?' Mrs. Brace murmured. 'Please, Sir Robert, I do understand. There is no need to explain. I have for some time realised, that although you consider me an enigma you cannot help being drawn to me. My absence only increased that feeling, and as you are probably also relieved that I have not met with an accident, or some such calamity, you expressed your relief in a manner customary to gentlemen in such a situation.'

Sir Robert stared at her in amazement. She really was the most extraordinary woman, which was probably why he found her so fascinating. For it had been her unorthodox manner which had first attracted him, and the reason that he now found her irresistible.

'So, Sir Robert,' she continued, without waiting for a response, 'I realise that in view of our new relationship, it is necessary for me to explain as much as I am able the reasons for my unusual behaviour.'

By now she had retreated to a seat on one side of the fireplace, so Sir Robert lowered himself somewhat unsteadily onto the one opposite.

'I believe my brother has already acquainted you with some of my past,' she began, 'but he knows only what I have been able to tell him with regard to the present, as to impart too much knowledge might put him in danger.' Sir Robert frowned and she nodded. 'Yes, Sir Robert, danger, for I have become involved in a very dangerous enterprise. But to commence at the beginning. Last year I was invited to Paris by Lord Stransbury, with whom you are acquainted. On my arrival he revealed to me that a plot had been discovered about a certain band of individuals, who were preparing plans to rescue Napoleon from St. Helena. There is apparently some unrest amongst those persons guarding the erstwhile Emperor, and he has been able with his charm and connivance, to persuade a young girl by name of Betsy Balcombe …'

'Balcombe,' Sir Robert exclaimed. 'Why that's …'

'…the name Lord Stransbury mentioned in his letter,' Mrs. Brace continued. 'Her father is William Balcombe, a superintendent of public sales for the East India Company, and Napoleon lodged in a pavilion at the bottom of the

Balcombes' garden prior to moving into his permanent residence. The Balcombes' admiration and respect for Napoleon would not normally be of concern to anyone, but unfortunately certain agents sympathetic to the ex-Emperor believe that they can persuade the family to assist in his rescue. This is, of course, quite absurd considering the location of St. Helena, but it has caused a great deal of insurrection amongst those misguided individuals, both French and English, sympathetic to Napoleon, and also as far as the English contingent are concerned, very unsympathetic to our present Royal family.'

'Good lord,' Sir Robert declared. 'But what on earth do these people intend? Do they want a Republic?'

'No, they want to restore the Stuart dynasty.'

'Jacobites! But surely they must know that since Henry Stuart's, or rather Cardinal York's, death in 1807 the Stuart line is extinct.'

'So those of us unaware of the intricate relationships of our erstwhile monarch's emotional life would like to think, but I fear that is not so. Although most intelligent people consider it immaterial, the fact is that Prince Charles Edward created his daughter Charlotte, the Duchess of Albany, and made her his heiress. However, the result of this inheritance meant that her natural son by Prince Ferdinand of Rohan, otherwise the Archbishop of Cambrai and known as Count Roehenstart, but actually christened Charles Edward Stuart was, according to those misguided people who support the Jacobite cause, the rightful heir to our country's throne.'

'But ...' Sir Robert began, only to be silenced by a gentle wave of Mrs. Brace's right hand.

'Please, Sir Robert, the hour grows speedily towards the children's evening meal, and I would like to finish my explanation before leaving. Where was I, ah yes, Rohenstart, who has seen military service in Russia, and worked in the household of Duke Alexander of Wurttemberg, during which time he was rendered insolvent by the failure of his bankers. He therefore fled to America from where, a year ago, he came to this country. His exact whereabouts are unknown, but he is believed to be somewhere in Scotland.'

'But I fail to understand what this man has to do with Napoleon's friendship with the Balcombes?'

'Ah, there you have the intricacies of the situation, Sir Robert. While intense interest of the authorities is being directed towards a possible incident on St. Helena, the misguided supporters of the Jacobite cause will have full sway without being hindered. Now you are aware of the complexities of the situation, Sir Robert, I fear I must withdraw to my domestic duties. However, there is one more matter relating to gifts. I understand Mrs. Honniton has responsibility for all the house staff, and Harold Sinclair looks after everyone else. However, there remains the children; I am assuming you will wish to take care of Edward, Lucy and Edgar, but may I assume responsibility for the others?'

Almost bewildered by the abrupt change of subject, Sir Robert tried to concentrate.

'Er … yes, I was going to give Edward his father's tie pin, and Lucy one of her mother's bracelets, but Edgar,' he hesitated. '… I am not sure what he would like. You see, being away from home …'

'That is easily solved,' Mrs. Brace replied briskly. 'He can have the puppy which I now understand I was supposed to be bringing back from my travels. Now, please excuse me, Sir Robert, I have a great deal to do.'

'Surely …' Sir Robert protested, rising quickly to his feet; but too late. The door was closing behind Mrs. Brace before he had a chance to complete his sentence.

He stared morosely at the closed door. How very feminine of her, to remind him of his attempt to pacify the children with a proverbial white lie.

But that was irrelevant compared to the majority of what she had said. Apart from imparting a complicated and highly irrational tale of two possible intrigues concerning two entirely different men who had no connection with each other, she had told him nothing. She had not even apologised for breaking into his desk; and what about the injuries she had acquired; and the grave desecrations, not to mention the violent attacks in and around Grosvenor Square? And what about that extraordinary book on the human body? Where did they all fit into this confusing and almost unbelievable narrative; and most important of all, what of her acknowledgement, and apparent acceptance of his interest?

Intensely irritated, yet annoyed with himself for caring, Sir Robert went to his room where he found Wenders laying out his evening wear. The sight of the valet reminded Sir

Robert that regardless of eccentric governesses, and the upheaval of his previously calm existence, the practicalities of life continued in their customary manner, and he found the thought soothing.

Neither man mentioned Mrs. Brace, and later that evening when Sir Robert retired to his library, he spent most of the time staring into the slowly dying embers, trying to decide how he should proceed emotionally with this unpredictable woman.

She was his employee, and as such under his protection, so any approach he made if he were to take such an action, had to be circumspect; and possibly through her brother. But what kind of an approach should he make? A proposal of marriage was the next correct procedure, but did he really know enough about her as an individual, to take such a monumental step? Granted, she was an educated, cultured woman of considerable intelligence, whom he found delightful and would have been heartbroken to lose; but was that enough? What of that other secret life, which demanded so much of her attention. The rigmarole she had narrated had concerned other people; and had given no indication of her involvement in either of the plots.

He sighed. Until she revealed some information with regard to her own activities, there was nothing further he could do so he made his way dejectedly upstairs.

As he was walking along the corridor, he realised that the twins had not visited him that evening to wish him good night. So changing direction, he turned a corner and walked quietly towards their bedroom. As he approached he heard Mrs. Brace's voice singing a lullaby, and for a few moments the years slipped away, and he was listening to his mother, as she sang him gently to sleep. He hesitated, then rather than disturb the tranquillity of the moment, he continued to his own room.

13

With Mrs. Brace's return all the amateur teachers were relieved of their duties, much to the relief of Wenders, who had found Edgar's questions with regard to Captain Cook and the reasons for his demise as a native lunch, somewhat difficult to answer.

'I tried to explain what a cannibal was, Sir Robert,' he said, 'but Master Edgar didn't seem to understand. He kept quoting the Old Testament and the food decreed by God as inedible.'

'Well, it's all over now,' Sir Robert reassured him. 'I am most obliged to you for your help; and I am sure now that Master Edgar has his puppy, nothing could be further from his mind than Captain Cook and his unfortunate end.'

The little dog had arrived just as everyone was about to enjoy the festivities, both religious and celebratory. But Sir Robert was not anticipating one aspect of the celebrations with his customary enthusiasm. After the festivities for the staff and village tenants, there would be the annual dinner and ball for those of Sir Robert's friends who owned the neighbouring estates. The event had always been attended with obvious enjoyment by everyone; although in Sir

Robert's opinion he had always considered his guests to be somewhat over-dressed for an indoor function.

However, it was not his guests' social attire that was concerning him, but the presence of Mrs. Brace. Since his sister-in-law's death, Sir Robert had always invited the most senior lady present to partner him when opening the ball. But that had been when there was no other eligible female living at Hawton; this was no longer the case, because there was now Mrs. Brace.

Sir Robert gave a deep sigh. In normal circumstances the governess would not even have been visible, but the present situation was far from normal. This particular governess, apart from also working as an agent for the government, had been passionately embraced by her employer without apparently any objection.

Although their embrace had been mentioned, Sir Robert still had no idea whether she considered it a passing impulse, or believed it to be a gesture signifying that their personal relationship was something more formal.

There was also the problem of what to give her for a present, or alternatively not to give her? Initially, he had decided to ignore the problem and behave as if it was natural not to give anything to a governess; but what if she gave him something? It was not likely but not impossible.

At last, in an effort to solve at least one situation, he decided to have a gift ready in case she gave him one. So he placed a pretty silver and pearl brooch, which had belonged to his late mother, in his desk drawer to await developments.

As to the other problem, Sir Robert decided, with some reluctance, to consult Wenders. His valet received the news with his customary pragmatism.

'I am sure my sister would be only too honoured to be included, Sir Robert. She is accustomed to mixing with all manner of gentry, especially since her sojourn in Paris. May I enquire, Sir Robert, would you prefer me to intimate your wishes?'

'Er… yes… I think that would be ... that is to say, yes, if you would be so kind,' Sir Robert replied, feeling suddenly rather heated.

It was the coward's way out of his dilemma, but at least it did not commit either of them in any way, and he hoped Mrs. Brace would view the situation accordingly.

However, there was still the question of her possible gift, and in an attempt to discover if she had procured anything for him, he enquired as to what she intended for the orphans.

'I have tried to reflect what I think is a part of their personality,'she explained. 'For instance, for Jack, whose particular interest is history, I have chosen an ornate book listing all England's monarchs since King Alfred; Matthew, who complained recently that it was a pity horses could not be ridden inside, will receive a hobby-horse; Timothy, who is very adept at drawing, a small easel with a set of crayons; while Mark, whose writing ability has proved exceptional a set of stencil sheets for copying.'

'Very appropriate,' Sir Robert muttered. 'Er ... and that is all?'

'All Sir Robert ? I fear I do not comprehend.'

'Of course not.' Sir Robert shook his head. 'Forgive me, I am getting confused.'

'Certainly, there is a lot to think about,' Mrs. Brace replied with a smile, as she left the room.

Whether it was the children's obvious pleasure on receiving their gifts, or the ceremonial lighting of the yule log, that made Sir Robert remember with affection the family celebrations of his childhood he did not know. All he was aware of was the sense of happiness which seemed to pervade the house, and everyone in it.

The 25th December commenced dry with bright sunlight, making the traditional walk to church a pleasure instead of an ordeal. Sir Robert led the way, followed by Mrs. Brace and the children, with the Hawton Hall staff bringing up the rear in order of seniority.

Afterwards, all the villagers and the residents of the Hall gathered in the dining hall for lunch, while anyone who could play an instrument indulged themselves with music for the villagers to dance to.

When at last the final villager had left, Sir Robert changed into his evening clothes, prior to receiving his guests. As usual these included Lord and Lady Alton, an elderly childless couple; Sir Simon and Lady Kay, newcomers to the area, and their son and daughter; and the Disbies, a family comprising husband, wife, and eight unmarried offspring.

As he was about to descend the staircase Sir Robert heard a commotion from above, and looking up saw seven small heads gazing excitedly over the banister.

'Please, Uncle, can we have a look? Mrs. Brace said she thought it would be all right if we were very good, and didn't make a noise,' Edward pleaded.

Sir Robert nodded. After all, who was he to disagree with Mrs. Brace? Delighted that she had accepted his invitation to attend the dinner, he was intrigued to see whether she would appear clad in her customary subdued garb, or present herself dressed in evening clothes equal to the occasion. With Mrs. Brace anything was possible.

The first guests to arrive were the Rev. Carter and his family, and as was usual whenever they visited Hawton, they came well clad in scarves, cloaks and mufflers, which they immediately shed hurriedly on seeing the roaring fire in the hall.

This performance was repeated by all the guests, especially those who were well aware of Hawton's customary lack of heating. In fact, Lord Alton was heard to remark softly to his wife: 'He's had the place done up, don't ye know.' While Lord Disbie received a very sharp tap from his wife's fan when he muttered: 'The chimneys been swept, Maria. The smoke's going up, instead of out.'

As soon as everyone had arrived, Sir Robert led the way to the dining-hall where Mrs. Brace stood waiting; and if any of the guests considered it unusual to be greeted by the elegantly clad governess, they were too well bred to react in any way; although Lord Disbie was seen to glance significantly at his wife, as everyone took their place.

Sir Robert had taken the precaution of seating Mrs. Brace beside newcomer Sir Simon Kay, who appeared to accept the inclusion of the governess as part of the country ways he had yet to experience, and they were soon discussing the problems France was facing as it reconstructed itself after Napoleon's defeat.

'There is a rumour that friends are plotting his escape,' Sir Simon remarked.

'So I have heard,' Mrs. Brace replied. 'But I fear they will not succeed. St. Helena is almost mid-ocean, and any boat approaching or leaving can easily be seen. Besides, Sir Hudson Lowe is rumoured to be most assiduous in his duties as Governor.'

'You appear well informed, Madam. Do you take an interest in the politics of our day?'

'Not at all, Sir Simon,' Mrs. Brace smiled. 'It is all hearsay, I assure you. But Napoleon caused such havoc the last time he escaped, I am merely assuming that this time extra care will be taken to avoid such a calamity again. May I enquire as to how you are adjusting to rural life, as I believe you moved here only recently?'

'Indeed, both my wife and I could not be better served. London's many charms were beginning to pall. Due primarily to the increase in crime, especially those relating to the desecrated graves, which Lady Kay found most distressing. The peace and tranquillity of country living has restored her to good health, and I find the neighbourhood also suits me very well.'

They were both sitting halfway down the table, some six people distant from where Sir Robert was seated at the top, but both Mrs. Brace's clear tones and Sir Simon's strong male voice reached his ears just as the governess was denying any official knowledge on the subject of the ex-Emperor.

He glanced sharply at her. Had she deliberately introduced the topic of Napoleon to distract Sir Simon, and if so, why? Sir Robert examined his guest. The Kays had moved into the district some six months previously, and so far as Sir Robert was aware Sir Simon was not in the habit of making unexpected visits to London, nor did he keep carrier pigeons.

Sir Robert turned to Lady Kay who, as this was her first visit to Hawton Hall, was seated by her host.

'And does your ladyship share Sir Simon's interest in the ex-Emperor?' he asked.

She gave a little laugh. 'Indeed no, Sir Robert, and neither really does my husband. He was in Paris for some time prior to Napoleon's escape from Elba, and is only too glad that there is no possibility of another such fiasco.'

'How interesting. May I ask, was his position governmental?'

'I am afraid I cannot say. I did not go with him due to my health at the time, and he was forced to leave France when he heard of Napoleon's escape.'

Sir Robert was going to pursue the subject, when he caught Mrs. Brace staring somewhat fixedly at him. For some reason, it was obvious she did not want him to continue. So, instead, he concentrated on explaining the various improvements he had made to the house.

It was during a lull in the conversation that Sir Robert realised how very relaxed and contented he felt, and he glanced around at his guests. Most of the men, when young, had shared in his boyhood pursuits, and he had learned to ride, hunt, and fish in their company.

With the exception of Merton, and possibly Randall, few of his London acquaintances would have considered such a way of life beneficial to their social welfare. Without attending Almacks' over-heated rooms and countless visits to the opera or theatre, none of his city friends would have considered their days endurable.

As the ball had been arranged to follow immediately after dinner, the ladies did not retire to leave the gentlemen to their port; instead all the guests made their way to the ballroom, from where they could hear the orchestra already playing.

Very quickly the younger guests had taken their partners and commenced the first dance, while the older guests either soon joined them or seated themselves around the room to converse, and watch.

It was while Sir Robert was escorting Lady Kay onto the floor that he noticed Mrs. Brace appeared to be missing. Assuming that she had gone up to the nursery to supervise her charges, he tried to concentrate on his partner, while trying to reassure himself that his governess had not made yet another of her immediate departures.

It was nearly two in the morning before Sir Robert, having bid his last guests goodnight and dismissed his staff, was able to ascertain whether Mrs. Brace was still in the house. Glancing into the various rooms allocated to the children he found only contented sleepers while the governess's own chamber was empty.

Apprehensively retracing his steps down to the ballroom, he tried to decide what to do. It was too late to rouse everyone for a search party, so he tried to convince himself that she might have gone out to examine her pigeon loft.

Then he heard a slight sound, and pushing open the ballroom doors, discovered Mrs. Brace, obviously unaware of his presence, waltzing elegantly about the floor to a tune she was humming softly.

Sir Robert stood motionless, until turning, she saw him, and smiling held out her hands.. Very aware that his heart appeared to be thumping at an alarming rate, Sir Robert walked across the floor and took his governess in his arms.

How long they waltzed gently around the room Sir Robert had no idea. But what he did know was that at the end of her humming, it seemed perfectly natural that they should hold each other very close, before exchanging a kiss that seemed to last forever.

14

The wintry sunshine was already beginning to penetrate Sir Robert's bedroom, and the fire was emitting a warm glow when he awoke the next morning. For a few moments he lay motionless, before extending a tentative arm to his left; it encountered only an empty space.

Although relieved to avoid the obvious embarrassment of Wenders discovering his sister in his master's bed, Sir Robert also felt bereft that the woman who last night had agreed to be his wife had, apparently, now deserted him. But it was only her physical presence that was lacking; the memories of her responses to his passion were as vivid as if she were still in his arms.

Suddenly aware that by now Wenders should have appeared with hot chocolate and water for shaving, Sir Robert flung back his covers as, simultaneously, there was a sharp knock on his door.

'Enter,' he called, noting as he did so that his voice sounded particularly enthusiastic. Then he stared in surprise, for the servant who entered his room was not Wenders, but the head footman, Charles Henderson.

'Mr. Wenders sends sincere apologies, Sir Robert,' he said with a nervous expression, 'but an urgent message arrived very early this morning for Mrs. Brace and Mr. Wenders, and they both had to leave.'

'Leave!' Sir Robert's exclamation was so resounding, members of Hawton's staff working on the ground floor hurried to the kitchens below to be out of harm's way.

'Er ... yes, Sir Robert. Mrs. Brace left you a note, and Mr. Wenders said I was to tell you to look out for the pigeons but ...'

It was only Sir Robert's well-bred self-control that held in check his desire to smash his unfortunate messenger to the ground.

'Thank you,' he managed, in a voice that seemed to slice through the air. 'You have Mrs. Brace's note?'

He held out his hand, as Henderson hurriedly extracted a packet from his pocket.

'Thank you, I'll shave myself this morning and you can lay out my riding clothes, as I shall probably go out after breakfast.'

Once inside his washroom Sir Robert opened Mrs. Brace's message. Whatever confused feelings he had were soon replaced by ones of concern and anger. Concern for her safety, and anger that Wenders had apparently allowed her, yet again, to behave outlandishly. For the note read:

My Dearest Love, Please forgive me for deserting you, but my brother awoke me with a message from London to which I have had to respond by leaving for town at once. It would seem that evil people are

152

gaining power and as I have certain knowledge, which because of its seriousness cannot be conveyed by letter, I must take it in person. Believe me when I say that leaving you is the very hardest action of my life, especially after the love and words we exchanged last night. You have done me the very greatest honour by asking me to be your wife, and I can only say how much I look forward to sharing my life with you. Perhaps it will ease your mind to know that I am not alone, as Arnold insisted on accompanying me to ensure my safety during the journey. I will send you a message via pigeon as soon as I reach town, and I look forward, my dearest love, to seeing you again very soon. With all my heart, your own Amanda.

Unfortunately, Mrs. Brace's assurances that her brother would be her protector did nothing to reassure Sir Robert whatsoever.

'Ease my mind,' he muttered to himself. 'The man's confessed he can't use a sword, and I shouldn't imagine he's any better with a gun.'

Some hours later, having examined the pigeons and found nothing of relevance and with his mind still a turmoil of emotions, Sir Robert decided regardless of the consequences to follow Mrs Brace, or Amanda as he now regarded her, and if possible assist her in whatever way he could.

To do this he would have to leave the children behind, and for a few moments he hesitated. But after having been assured by Mrs. Honniton that she would look after them and make sure they did the lessons Mrs. Brace had already arranged, Sir Robert ordered his carriage to be prepared for an immediate journey to London.

Realising his departure should appear as natural as possible, despite it still being the Christmas season, Sir Robert let it be known that his lawyer had that day sent a message by pigeon, regarding certain urgent financial matters that had to be settled immediately.

'I won't be gone long,' he said reassuringly to the children, as they stood on Hawton's steps to wave goodbye. 'And I want you all to do as Mrs. Honniton tells you and, remember, don't go near the lake again until I return.'

There was a chorus of assent and then, after one last look at the seven rather concerned little faces, Sir Robert climbed into the carriage. Unaware of what might await him in London he decided to take Henderson, in addition to Rivers Newsome and Sam Bridges, as all three men were physically strong, and all expert shots and experienced swordsmen.

Obliged to break their journey in order to renew their horses, Sir Robert spent an anxious night pacing his room until, both physically and mentally exhausted, he lay down and dozed fitfully until dawn.

He arrived in Grosvenor Square during a heavy fall of snow, and all four men were so cold Symons had the staff scurrying about building up fires and administering hot drinks.

But while the others indulged gratefully, Sir Robert waved aside the steaming bowl offered by Walter, and instead demanded to know whether Mrs. Brace or Wenders were in the house. The footman shook his head.

'No, Sir Robert, they have not returned, but Mr. Best might know where they are. A message was delivered a few hours ago which he said was for you.'

'For me,' Sir Robert exclaimed. 'I must see Best at once.'

Walter flushed in obvious embarrassment. 'I'm afraid he's not here at the moment, Sir Robert. As soon as he got the message he went out, and I don't think he's yet returned. Perhaps Mr. Symons …'

But Sir Robert was out in the hallway before the unfortunate footman had time to finish his sentence.

Trying to keep his voice as natural as possible, Sir Robert asked Symons whether he knew, either when Best was expected to return, or where he might be at that moment.

'I must apologise, Sir Robert, but I have no idea. Mr. Best left the house in great haste without saying anything.'

'And you have heard nothing from either Mrs. Brace, or her … that is, Wenders?'

'No, I fear not, Sir Robert,' Symons replied abjectly.

His initial anger and frustration slowly changing into concern and bewilderment, Sir Robert retreated to his library, and sinking into a chair tried to decide what to do.

He felt as if he had fallen into a gigantic maze, out of which there seemed to be no exit. Where were Amanda and Wenders, and who had sent what was most likely the bogus message which Best had answered? Then Sir Robert remembered his vow to avenge Jack's treatment by Mick Taylor.

'At least,' he thought. 'Finding him would give me something to do.'

As to what exactly he would do if he succeeded in finding his quarry, Sir Robert was somewhat vague: there was no law prohibiting children being placed as apprentices to learn a trade, regardless of how menial or dangerous the work.

Thinking of his four little waifs at Hawton, Sir Robert felt suddenly ashamed. Despite his interest in poor and abandoned children, he had never spoken out publicly against the atrocities that he knew some of them were forced to endure. His association with his new charges illustrated overwhelmingly the wide social gap that existed, between those with money and status, and the poor and impotent.

Although all his staff, retainers and tenants knew he could be relied on for their welfare, the gap between employer and employee was too immense. So he decided when the present situation had been resolved, and life had returned to something like normal, he would have to try and make radical changes for the better. But for the time being he would concentrate on finding Mike Taylor, and seeing if he could bring him to justice.

Rising from his seat, Sir Robert strode towards the library door but before he reached it the house resounded with loud knocking sounds. Stepping into the hallway Sir Robert was appalled to see William Best, his face bruised and bleeding, being helped into the house by Radcliff and Mr. Symons.

'In heaven's name, man, what's happened?' Sir Robert exclaimed.

'It was the note, Sir Robert, from Lord Randall,' Best gasped. 'I decided it was urgent, and as you were not here I went instead and was set upon by some ruffians.'

'But why should Lord Randall request my company. He would not have known I had returned to London,' Sir Robert protested. 'And to where were you directed?'

'A house off Houndsditch, Sir Robert, and if I had not been armed I think they would have killed me and …'

'Forgive me for interrupting, Sir Robert,' Symons interjected. 'But I think it necessary for Mr. Best to be attended to.'

'Yes, of course,' Sir Robert replied hurriedly. 'But did you retain the note, Best?'

The steward nodded, and as he stumbled away between his helpers Sir Robert unfolded a creased piece of paper. It was very brief:

Robert I am in Stoney Lane off Houndsditch and need your immediate assistance. George

Perplexed, Sir Robert stared at the handwriting which was a tolerable copy of his friend's, but the writer had obviously been unaware that gentlemen never used first names, but always addressed and signed their missives with surnames.

Undecided whether to continue with his original plan to trace Mike Taylor, or go to Stoney Lane and investigate who had sent him the note, Sir Robert was interrupted by a discreet cough from his senior footman.

'Begging your pardon, Sir Robert, but Chef was wondering if you would like some lunch? We gather from Mr. Bridges that you haven't eaten since early this morning. And would you care to refresh yourself first, Sir Robert. In Mr. Wenders' absence, I have taken the liberty of laying out some washing materials in your room and also a change of garments.'

Relieved to be brought back to the more mundane activities of life, Sir Robert nodded.

'Yes indeed, no matter the situation one's life continues like the proverbial wheel. Thank you, Walter, but I am anxious to seek out Lord Randall, as he may be in some difficulty. So I will change and eat later, and can you arrange for Newsome to saddle three horses as I would like him to accompany me, together with Henderson and Bridges.'

Anxious to set out on his journey, Sir Robert was soon trotting through Grosvenor Square closely followed by his three companions, all of whom were armed. When at last they reached Stoney Lane, they discovered it was one of a number of narrow streets off Houndsditch, full of poorly constructed houses, all of which appeared deserted. Stopping at the one described by Best, Sir Robert leaned down and knocked on the door with his riding crop.

After two more attempts, he was about to seek out Mike Taylor when Henderson pointed towards a window above the front door.

'There's some movement against the glass, Sir Robert,' he said. 'As if someone is trying to attract our attention.'

Within minutes, Newsome and Bridges had forced the door open, and the four men were mounting a rickety staircase at the top of which there was another door. As they hesitated, they heard a muffled sound and on pushing their way into the room found Lord Randall, his mouth gagged and his face badly bruised, wearing only a shirt and breeches both of which were heavily soiled and torn.

'George!' Sir Robert exclaimed in astonishment. 'What in heaven's name are you doing here?'

'Robert, thank God,' Lord Randall gasped, as soon as his gag had been removed. 'I'm so sorry your man was injured, but if he had not put up such a good fight it might have been worse.'

'But what is happening? Why are you here and in this state? Surely ... '

'Sir Robert, forgive me, sir,' Newsome interrupted. 'But I think we should get Lord Randall out of this place and take him home to recover. He appears to be in a very bad way.'

'Yes, yes, of course,' Sir Robert agreed hurriedly. 'I'm so sorry, George, of course you must be attended to as soon as possible. Can you ride? If so, let Henderson take you home and ... '

'No, not my home,' Lord Randall gasped. 'I don't want Madeleine to see me like this. Can I go to Grosvenor Square and let your people attend to me? I would be most obliged.'

'Yes, yes, most certainly,' Sir Robert replied. 'Come along, let's get you downstairs and out of this pest hole.'

15

It was over an hour before Sir Robert was able to question his friend, as Lord Randall had fainted on arriving in Grosvenor Square and a surgeon had to be summoned to ensure he had not sustained a serious injury, in addition to the abrasions and bruises on his body.

When at last Sir Robert was allowed into Lord Randall's room, he was concerned to see how exhausted his friend was, but as soon as they were alone Lord Randall sighed heavily.

'Firstly, I must apologise, Robert. I had no intention of involving you, but if you had not rescued me I doubt I would have survived. Amanda told me she had explained some of the details to you, but these people are so ruthless in their determination to attain their objective they will stoop to any infamy necessary.'

'So I gather; and where, incidentally, are my governess and her brother?'

'Why, are they not at Hawton?' Lord Randall asked, looking surprised.

'No, apparently she received a message by pigeon post telling her something, I have no idea what, and that this made it imperative she should return to London.'

'Good God, Robert, and you've no idea where she's gone?'

'Not the slightest, but she seems very capable of defending herself, despite her unfortunate encounter last year.'

'You don't understand,' Lord Randall's voice rose slightly. 'These people are utterly ruthless, and killing or maiming is part of their regime. You saw what they did to your servant, and what they've done to me. If Amanda and her brother are somewhere in London, they could be in danger. You'll have to get in touch with Demonds, and tell him what has happened. He might know where they are.'

'Demonds?'

'Yes, that's not his real name obviously, but he knows all the secret addresses that we use. Whereas most of us only know the ones we work from. How much has Amanda actually told you?'

'That there are some quite mad individuals who wish to restore the Stuart dynasty which, considering the number of eligible descendents of his present Majesty, I find quite ludicrous.'

'Unfortunately it is due to those descendants that the idea was proposed in the first place.'

'But ...' began Sir Robert, only to be interrupted by Lord Randall.

'My dear friend, consider the situation with regard to the present incumbents of our royal house. King George is insane and locked away in Windsor. His heir is a profligate over-indulged individual, who refuses to acknowledge his wife. While his heiress, delightful though she may be, is known to be delicate and hardly likely to survive the child she is carrying. This leaves the remainder of the Prince Regent's many brothers, all of whom are even more stupid and dissolute than him. Similar to one of Mr. Shakespeare's tragedies, the scene is set, and the play is proceeding to its inexorable end. These Jacobeans, as they call themselves, are poised ready to advance; and considering that the majority of our present population have little or nothing and resent the existence of those who have everything, rousing a jealous mob would not be difficult. Small groups of usurpers are already littered around the capital and surrounding country areas, and when called upon they will strike in such a way that the ignorant public will be almost unaware of what is happening.'

'But the constables, the government ...' Sir Robert began.

'There are seven members of Parliament and six Lords amongst these felons, and at least a small contingent of the so-called constable fraternity. As to the public, a number of them, I fear, have already been persuaded, with promises of financial gain, to join this motley band. It is these ruffians who have been desecrating graves and attacking innocent members of the public, in order to divert constabulary attention. We suspected this, but it was not until Amanda followed a band of them to Newgate and saw them at work in a Newgate cemetery, that we discovered our suspicions were correct. That was the night she was attacked by one of these blackguards, a particularly repellent individual, by name Mick Taylor.'

'Good Lord,' Sir Robert declared. 'That's the man I've come to London to find. He makes a living by selling young boys into what amounts to slavery; and I have vowed to bring him to justice . But how did Amanda manage to return to Grosvenor Square from Newgate?'

'Over the rooftops, and she was fortunate to meet one of our friends on the way; he helped her across the city. Without his assistance, she might have succumbed to her injury. Now my friend, you know almost all and please delay your act of revenge until later. As first we must contact Demonds, and discover Amanda's whereabouts. He is a lawyer with chambers in Lincoln's Inn. Give me some writing materials and I will give you the address. I suggest you call yourself Palmer. As I said before, we all use pseudonyms. Mine's Stone, and Amanda is known as Westerley. Clothe yourself simply and hire a vehicle, don't ride. You have to appear as insignificant as possible. Oh, and could you kindly leave a note with Madeleine. She may be worrying by now, but if I write that I am with you it will calm any concerns she might have.'

'How much does she know?'

'That was very difficult,' Lord Randall replied, looking concerned. 'She knew I was involved in something which I could not reveal, and that my untoward behaviour was false, but the fact that I managed to persuade everyone that I had deteriorated into an alcoholic boor, reflected on her and that concerned me greatly. I was also worried about Edgar. Which was why I asked you to take him to Hawton, and I understand from Amanda that he has really thrived down there.'

'Yes, we both made sure he was given every possible opportunity to enjoy himself; and I understand that Madeleine is quite happy for his friend Jack to join your household?'

'Forgive me,' Lord Randall said looking contrite. 'I've never thanked you properly for having Edgar, and for doing so much for him. He's always been a rather lonely lad, and we are both delighted that he has made a friend. Madeleine tells me that Jack has had some sort of education, and is not just a waif from the streets like his companions. Here, dear friend, is my note to Madeleine, and may I suggest one of your servants takes it. If I am supposed to be spending time with you, I would hardly be delivering my own correspondence.'

Later, having borrowed some garments from Newsome, since none of his own were considered by Lord Randall to be suitable, Sir Robert made his way across London to Lincoln's Inn Fields. The house was a tall austere-looking building with dirty windows and chipped paintwork, and the response to Sir Robert's knock seemed to echo through the building as if it were empty.

At last, after what seemed to be an eternity, there was the sound of a key turning and a bolt being pulled back, after which the door opened slowly to reveal a very small girl carrying a rather large doll. Expecting to see at least a fully grown figure, Sir Robert stared down in surprise and then said the only thing he could think of under the circumstances.

'Is your Mama in?'

The child shook her head. 'No but Papa is here. Do you want him?'

Before Sir Robert could reply, a stentorian voice from somewhere inside yelled:

'Isabella, close the door.'

Obediently, the girl began to push the door to and it was only because it happened to be particularly heavy for such small hands to manipulate, that Sir Robert managed to slide into the hallway.

The inside of the building looked even dustier and more neglected, than the exterior, and the elegantly clad child looked incongruous amongst such squalor.

'Isabella, what has Papa told you, you must NOT answer the door.' The speaker, an agitated, rather dishevelled but otherwise well-dressed young man carrying a naked sword, ran swiftly down the stairs, from where he approached Sir Robert with obvious caution.

'Mr. Demonds?' Sir Robert asked, glancing askance at the weapon. 'Er ... I am Palmer, I come from Stone.'

'Ah, yes,' Demonds nodded, lowering his sword. 'But let us go to the back. I hope no one saw you arrive, and Isabella, please do not answer the door ever again.'

But the recipient of this repeated admonition was already trotting along the corridor, apparently oblivious to her parent's concern.

'Do you have children, sir?' Without waiting for a reply the young man sighed heavily. 'I love her dearly, but she will insist on accompanying me and it can become very difficult. Her mother, my dear wife ...'

'I am so sorry,' Sir Robert murmured sympathetically, where upon the young man shook his head energetically.

'No, no, she's not dead, indeed no. She's enceinte with our second child, which is why I have Isabella.'

'Perhaps a nurse?' Sir Robert murmured.

'I fear dear Matilda is not sympathetic to nurses, and as she requires a great deal of rest at this particular time, I have no alternative but to bring Isabella with me.'

By this time they had reached what appeared to be a small sitting-room at the back of the house, and Sir Robert was pleased to see, that unlike the rest of the building, the room was clean and the furniture well polished.

'Now, I am assuming Stone has enlightened you as to my position?' Demonds looked enquiringly at Sir Robert.

'Yes, Lord ...'

Demonds frowned.. 'Please remember, no real names; it's too dangerous. Now to explain. I sent the pigeon message to your country house, because we needed Westerley to find out the present situation regarding Merton.'

'Merton? You are not referring to David Merton?' Sir Robert exclaimed.

'Why yes, didn't you know? He is one of the leaders of their gang; for that's what it is and one of the most ruthless. You may have heard that a servant called Meggie Sullivan disappeared from his London home. He has insisted she just absconded; but the truth is that the poor girl discovered his villainy somehow, and he had her disposed of. One of his many grave desecrators attended to her remains, which were disfigured beyond recognition. That is all I can tell you at the moment, and I will write a note for Stone as to Westerley's whereabouts. She's quite safe, and will no doubt tell you herself where she has been when next you meet. I would recommend you depart by the back entrance, and then continue into the nearest high street from where you should be able to procure some form of conveyance.'

Three hours later, having returned home and given Demonds' note to Lord Randall, Sir Robert retired to his library. The revelation with regard to David Merton had shaken him considerably, and he found it very difficult to believe it was true. They had known each other since boyhood, when Lord Merton had been a frequent visitor to Hawton. They had also shared the various complications of school life together, and Sir Robert had been Merton's Chief Groom at his wedding.

As his mind ran through the many times he had talked with David Merton, Sir Robert now realised that politics had never featured greatly in their conversation, and they had certainly never discussed the legitimacy of the Royal family, nor their right to rule. In fact, as he now reflected, Sir Robert realised that during the past two or three years their conversation had been limited mainly to mundane matters such as hunting or horse racing, and minor problems that Lord Merton might be experiencing on his estate.

Why Lord Merton had acquired such radical views with regard to his politics Sir Robert could not imagine, and had it not been for George Randall recovering upstairs from his wounds and the remembrance of the attack on Amanda, Sir Robert felt that he might have been caught up in a theatrical farce, similar to those now being enjoyed by the more uneducated of the population.

Hearing the sound of a carriage drawing up outside, Sir Robert opened the library door to discover Symons admitting Lady Randall, Amanda, and a dishevelled and exhausted-looking Wenders.

16

Two hours later, having convinced a horrified Madeleine Randall that her husband was not about to meet his Maker and assured Wenders that he should retire to his room to recover, Sir Robert and Amanda sat together in the library, where he disclosed all that occurred between himself and Demonds. Having given her the latter's message, Sir Robert stared at her accusingly.

'Where did you go, and what for heaven's sake happened to your brother to leave him in such a state?'

'One at a time,' Amanda shook her head with a laugh. 'I explained in my note that there was a problem, but what I could not reveal was that it involved the grave desecrations. The agent who had been on the watch had been observed, so he had to depart at speed leaving no one on guard. I had to replace him with someone else, and to do that I had to come to London. I knew, if I had awoken you, you would have insisted on accompanying me, and that would have presented difficulties as it would have meant embroiling you in our plans. So instead, as Arnold was concerned at the thought of me travelling yet again alone to the city he accompanied me. But unfortunately he is not an accomplished rider, so I recommend he is given time to recover as he was in the saddle nearly all day.'

'Of course, but what of your colleagues; would I know any of the others apart from Demonds? I find it hard to believe that I could have been so completely duped by David Merton. Is it truly possible that he was responsible for that poor girl's death?'

'I fear so, and that is something for which I am deeply ashamed; for it was at my suggestion that she applied for the post of governess. At first George protested, saying it as too dangerous, for Merton is no fool, but Meggie insisted she would be careful; and knowing how proficient she was, for she has worked for us before, it was at my insistence that George agreed. I know not how she died, only that her mangled body was discovered by a constable, washed up on the Thames embankment near Richmond. To try and find out exactly what she had endured, I purchased that book that so alarmed you. If Merton were ever brought to trial, I wanted how he killed her to be clearly explained.' Amanda shook her head. 'He is indeed a devil.'

'Merciful God, what did he do to her?' Sir Robert gasped. 'And to think I have on occasions confided in that man; but what of Alice, surely she was not privy to such a horror? And who else is shielded by such a mask of hypocrisy? What of the Baberstocks, the Coopers, the Mancasters and the Bassengers, and all the others whom I have always considered friends?'

'The Mancasters are loyal royalists and so are the Baberstocks, but we are very concerned that the Kays have moved to the country and so near to Hawton Hall. Lord

Stransbury sent word that Sir Simon had been visiting someone in Edinburgh up to three months ago; but his spies were unable to discover the man's identity or what passed between them. At your dinner party I mentioned Napoleon deliberately to see his reaction. But if you remember, the subject was dismissed by both him and his wife. I do not suppose you have had any opportunity to discover why they decided to move to the area?'

'I hardly know them, apart from leaving my card when they took up residence. I invited them to dinner merely to assist them in meeting their neighbours.' He spread his arms wide in a gesture of despair. 'This whole situation is becoming like a complicated web. So am I to understand that the grave desecrations are merely a ruse, to distract the constabulary, while the Balcombes' efforts on St. Helena are likewise intended to distract those in national command?'

'Yes, that is a coincidence we did not anticipate; and as these good official folk direct their attention towards the deposed Emperor, the future Charles Stuart will be smuggled surreptitiously into the country to be launched on an unsuspecting population, no doubt with great violence against anyone opposing him.'

'Demonds explained how this was to succeed; but despite the violence you describe I find it hard to believe the majority of our honest citizens will simply accept a usurper. And what manner of man is he? Has anyone actually met him? Surely ...'

'My dear Robert, you are more than aware of the division in this country between rich and poor, and the degradation to which some poor souls have to stoop to obtain food for their children. Your own actions in such matters more than demonstrates your concern, but this situation is universal and the disquiet and bitterness of the humbler population is rife. Especially since the enclosures; and remember what the French populace achieved, with the revolution? As to the character of the usurper as you call him, his previous escapades seem to have drained him mentally as well as physically; he is now considered to be a rather weak individual who has chosen to live a quiet and uneventful life somewhere in the country outside Paris. Or at least did live in that area, because if our suspicions are correct he may now be in Edinburgh. But now you must excuse me as I wish to speak to George. Ah no, just one other matter, dearest. I trust I may invite Madeleine to dine?'

Without waiting for a reply and in her traditional style Amanda then hurried from the room, leaving Sir Robert staring after her. As the door closed he sank back into his chair feeling somewhat dazed.

Apart from a tender embrace on arrival, she had given no indication that her status in his house had undergone a radical change. As his affianced wife she was now the future mistress of his home, and he felt slightly aggrieved that she seemed to have accepted this so calmly and without further preamble.

However, after a while he glanced up again at his mother's serene features and then smiled to himself. Without realising it, he had chosen for his wife a woman whose personality was almost identical to that of the late

Lady Masters which, on consideration, was not surprising, since his own personality strongly resembled that of his father.

This quiet, rather self-effacing man Sir Robert remembered as a warm demonstrative parent, whose greatest pleasure had been to read to his two young sons from one of their favourite books, had never been known to disagree with his wife or raise his voice in protest at some of her more unusual requests.

On reflection, Sir Robert realised that if his mother had not organised the Masters family so efficiently and arranged for their visits to the various fashionable entertainments, they would probably have vegetated into a state of mental decline in the same way that Hawton had deteriorated into a physical one.

And how enthusiastically both his parents would have welcomed Amanda. His mother because of her delight that he had at last formed the attachment for which she had so longed; and his father because of the bemused interest he would have expressed on realising that his future daughter-in-law was as unpredictable as his own wife.

Later that evening, after dinner, Sir Robert visited Lord Randall again to see how he was progressing.

'Fairly well old man, thank you, Your servants have been most helpful, and the surgeon thinks I may be able to return home tomorrow. I don't suppose you have heard any more news?'

'I'm afraid not.' Sir Robert frowned. 'Amanda has really only repeated what I've already learned from you and Demonds. But when is everything going to commence?

Does anyone know when this Jacobean usurper is going to journey down from his Scottish retreat?'

'Unfortunately no, but we have spies everywhere, and as soon as they really suspect the enemy is about to reveal himself we shall be told.'

Sir Robert crossed to the window. The moon was full and its brightness seemed to light up the whole of the square.

'I can't understand how you can be so calm,' he said. 'And this waiting around seems pointless to me. Surely there should be some sort of preparation? What about weapons, and when will you all gather somewhere to protect the royal family?'

'In a situation such as this, there is always a lot of patience required. But my dear fellow why don't you go down to the ladies? I'm sure they would be delighted to have your company.'

'With great respect to your dear wife, and my future wife ... Yes George, you will soon be receiving an invitation to a wedding, 'though I would be grateful if you could kindly keep the matter secret for the time being. Where was I? Oh yes, with great respect to the ladies I have decided to continue with the reason why I originally decided to return to London, and somehow track down Mick Taylor.'

'Taylor!' Lord Randall declared. 'But he's one of their gang.'

'So I understand. But he also happens to be the blackguard who makes a living by selling helpless children to chimney sweeps. Young Jack, the lad you will be taking into your home was one such child; and I have vowed, somehow or other, to avenge him.'

'How, in heaven's name?' Lord Randall stared at his friend in amazement. 'First of all you've got to find him and London is a very ...'

'Oh, I know where he lives. Jack told me he was a near neighbour of himself and his mother. So I shall go to Stepney and question some of the local folk as to Taylor's exact address.'

'That won't be easy, the poor and under-privileged have a kind of loyalty to each other. I fear you will have trouble questioning them. And when, or rather if you find him, what then?'

Sir Robert shrugged. 'Find a law officer I suppose, and get him convicted. I can use Jack as a witness and any of his neighbours who will help.'

'I wish you luck, but you won't find it a pleasant endeavour.'

'Maybe not,' Sir Robert replied grimly. 'But I shall try.'

Having made his decision, Sir Robert ordered Symons to tell Newsome, Bridges and Henderson, to prepare four horses and be ready to leave within an hour.

'And tell them to bring their muskets,' he added. 'But please don't let anyone else know, especially the ladies.'

Due to heavy early evening traffic, the journey to Stepney took longer than Sir Robert had anticipated, and it was early dusk by the time they reached Jack's old home.

The man who answered to Henderson's sharp tap on the door stared at his four visitors in surprise.

'Why, Your Honours, what can old Ben do for you. I ain't got any money or goods of any sorts. And if you're the officers, I ain't no thief either.'

'No, no,' Sir Robert said hurriedly. 'We are simply seeking out a fellow by name Mick Taylor. We came here first because I believe young Jack Fullerton used to live here with his mother?'

'Aye, that he did, and it were a bad business that it were. Dragged off he was and by yon Mick Taylor, as you say you're looking for. And his poor mother not cold she weren't, but Taylor he just didn't care. Wanted his money he did and her left unburied.'

'Did she ... that is ... did someone take care of her?' Sir Robert asked, trying to keep the anger out of his voice.

'Aye, that they did. Young Vicar, he took her and she were buried in Stepney churchyard. Afterwards, we all tried to find out what'd happened to young Jack, but Taylor, he wouldna say. So we don't know where he is, and he were such a nice lad. Cut above others around here, because his mother, she were a lady she were.'

Some time later, having obtained the vicar's address from the old man, Sir Robert dismounted before what might have once been an elegant manse, but which was now in great need of renovation.

Leaving his companions to refresh themselves at a local hostelry, Sir Robert gave the metal knocker on the Manse door a hearty thud. The response was the sound of running feet then a cry: 'I'll go, Mama.' After which, the door opened to reveal a young boy holding onto the collar of a ferocious-looking Alsatian.

'Down, Tabs, for goodness sake, it's a gentleman.' The boy gave a heave on the dog's collar by way of emphasis, but Tabs obviously had a mind of her own and continued to snarl. 'I am so very sorry, sir, but it's her puppies. She thinks you're going to take them away. She's very protective.'

Experiencing a distinct sense of deja vu, Sir Robert was about to enquire whether there was a parent in residence, when a cultured female voice echoed from somewhere within the house.

'Thomas, what are you doing at the door. Let the gentleman in.'

A few minutes later, Tabs having been hauled back to supervise the care of her offspring, Sir Robert introduced himself to the vicar's wife, Mrs. Irons, and explained the reason for his visit.

'Oh yes, poor Mrs. Fullerton, as she called herself. Her real name was Lesley, Dorothy Lesley. It was a disgrace what happened to the boy, and the trouble is that no one now knows where he is.'

'He is safe and well,' Sir Robert replied, gently. 'He was with a sweep who was hired to clean my chimneys, and when I saw what a state the child was in I ... well, I have to admit I bought him.' He flushed heavily. 'Not that I approve of such an action, but I had no intention of letting him go back to that life.'

'Not at all,' Mrs. Irons declared. 'That was an act of kindness because you have certainly saved his life. He was a delicately brought up child.' She hesitated. 'His mother was a lady, you see. And only living in this area because she could afford no other. Her history is a sad one, but I am very much afraid typical of these times. She came from a village in Wiltshire, and her father was the local doctor. Apparently, one day a member of the nobility had a riding accident and Mrs. Fullerton, or Miss Lesley as she was then, assisted her father with the patient and sadly, because she knew nothing of his character, they formed an alliance.' Mrs. Irons sighed. 'He promised her marriage, and being much enamoured she allowed intimacies and, I regret to say, he left her enceinte. Unfortunately, she had no mother in whom to confide, her father being a widower. So being too ashamed to reveal her condition, she fled to London and lodged with old Ben. He was very good to her, and after Jack was born she took in sewing and became quite successful hereabouts. As soon as we realised she was so ill - an inflammation of the lungs which our doctor said was incurable - we agreed to look after Jack. But as you now know, he was taken away before we realised the poor woman was dead. So what we could not do for the living, we did for the dead; my husband buried her beneath a tree in the church burial ground. When you see Jack again, do tell him where she is, and if he ever wishes to see her grave please bring him to us.'

'Indeed I will, but do you know who the blackguard was who took such advantage of the poor girl.'

Mrs. Irons frowned. 'She never spoke of him, other than briefly when she imparted her tale; and although I do not know from where he came or lived, his last name was Merton. Why, sir, what ails you? You have gone very pale. You cannot know the man, surely?'

'Yes,' Sir Robert muttered, almost incoherently, 'I am very much afraid I do.

17

Later that night, Sir Robert returned to Grosvenor Square in a highly irritable state. Having made numerous fruitless enquiries regarding Mick Taylor's whereabouts, he had eventually to admit that to continue the search in such bad light would be pointless. He was also concerned that having discovered Merton was Jack's father, the revelation might affect the Randalls' decision to adopt him.

His irritation also increased on discovering that Amanda had been called away on one of her *errands,* after returning to the house for only a few minutes.

'Where the hell has she gone?' Sir Robert declared, flinging himself down on a chair in the guest room.

Lord Randall gave his friend a wary glance. 'I'm not sure, but she only went with Madeleine so it can't be anything serious. I think they've gone to get some clothes.'

'Clothes!' Sir Robert stared at his friend in amazement. 'You mean they've gone shopping at this time of night?'

'No, no,' Lord Randall replied hurriedly. 'They've gone to get more of my clothes, and some of Madeleine's. Because the doctor said it would be advisable if I stayed here rather than return home, at least for the while. If that is not inconvenient to you,' he finished lamely, with another wary glance.

'Of course not, you can stay as long as you like.' Sir Robert gave a deep sigh. 'This is all getting too much for me. Especially after what I've heard about Merton.'

By the time he had disclosed all that Mrs. Irons had revealed, both Amanda and Lady Randall had returned, and the four of them sat discussing the latest revelations.

'I have to confess I am somewhat devastated,' Sir Robert said. 'When I think how close I have been to that man. Closer in some ways than you and I, George,' he added with a wry grin. 'How deceptive can someone be? When I think how I confided in him, and took his advice in many matters, believing him to be more practical and rational than myself, while all the while he was not only totally immoral but also a murderer and a traitor.'

'And this poor girl he so abused,' Lady Randall declared. 'I wonder whether her family know of her fate.'

'I doubt it,' Sir Robert replied. 'If they did, they surely would have tried to find Jack.'

'Do you think after everything has been settled, we should try and seek out the boy's family?' Lord Randall said. 'Not that I have any objection to adopting him,' he added hurriedly. 'No child can be held responsible for their parents' misdeeds, but if he does have relatives who would like to care for him, I think they should have the opportunity of knowing he exists.'

'And if they do not,' Lady Randall added, 'the original arrangement still stands. especially as Edgar is so fond of him.'

That night, when everyone had retired to bed, Sir Robert was awoken by the sound of horses' hooves resounding through the square. Assuming it was a late night traveller, or a post boy with an urgent letter, he turned over in bed and snuggled down to continue his rest. But the sound of hooves only increased until, suddenly, they ceased and were followed by someone hammering violently on Sir Robert's front door.

Immediately, every fibre of the silent house seemed to awake and footsteps could be heard running up and down corridors and stairs, while from outside a man's voice repeatedly yelled Sir Robert's name.

Leaping from his bed, and pausing only to pull on a dressing gown, Sir Robert hurried down the stairs to find Demonds standing in the hall, mud splattered, gasping out something to Symons.

'Sir Robert, I must see Sir ... Oh thank God you're here and ...'

'For heaven's sake, man,' Sir Robert interrupted. 'Take a breath, and then tell me what's happened. You're covered in mud. Symons, send someone to look after Mr. Demonds' horse.'

By this time every occupant of the house was awake, and either crowding into the hall or leaning over the upstairs banisters; one of whom was Amanda who on seeing Demonds, hurried downstairs.

'What's happened?' she asked, sharply. 'Are they all right?'

'No,' he panted. 'I was too late. It's started, and they've taken over Hawton Hall and everyone in it, including all the children.'

At the mention of *Hawton Hall* and *children*, Sir Robert felt himself grow cold.

'What are you talking about, man?' he snapped. 'What's happened to the children, and what do you mean, taken over my house?'

Before Demonds could reply, Lord Randall's voice echoed from the first landing.

'So it's started, has it? Does everyone know?'

But Sir Robert was too concerned about his small relatives to pay any attention to Lord Randall.

'The children,' he repeated, heatedly. 'What do you mean they've taken over the children; and who are *they*?'

'I fear the revolution has started, dearest,' Amanda murmured, soothingly, 'and they appear to have chosen Hawton Hall as their headquarters.'

'Merciful heaven!' Sir Robert stared at her in horror. 'But my nephew and his sister, and all the other children; what has happened to them?'

'And Edgar,' Lord Randall's voice echoed through the house. 'What about Edgar?'

Before anyone could reply, there was a cry from the other side of the landing and Lady Randall's voice seemed even louder than her husband's.

'What do you mean? Have they harmed our son?'

'Hush, dear,' Amanda called. 'All the children are together, so Edgar will be no more conspicuous than any of the others.'

'Merton hates me, always has,' Lord Randall declared. 'I'm coming with you.'

Before anyone had a chance to remonstrate with him, he returned to his room closely followed by his wife.

'Now to details,' Amanda declared to Demonds. 'Do you know how many there are? And what of the house staff? Have they been taken prisoner?'

'We don't know,' he replied. 'All we do know is that someone sent a pigeon message telling us what had happened. Apparently, someone called Kay led a party of men to Hawton and they overpowered all your people, Sir Robert, and have threatened to harm the children, if the staff don't obey their orders.'

Sir Robert, his complexion ashen, sat down heavily on the nearest seat.

'Kay,' he muttered. 'My new neighbour. You had your suspicions, didn't you, Amanda?'

'Yes, dearest,' she replied calmly. 'But this is what we have all been preparing for. So now we must call everyone out, and ride to the vicinity of Hawton Hall as soon as possible. Our only advantage, at the moment, is that we have more support than do the others. Godfrey, you go out and commence the chain, and I will send pigeons out to the Wilsons, the Gadstones and all the others, to rally at Chelsea village within the hour.

Bewildered by her abruptness, and thinking only of his nephew and niece, Sir Robert sat staring helplessly as Amanda returned quickly up the stairs, and Demonds rushed out of the house with the same speed he had entered it.

Lost in his momentary apathy, Sir Robert was hardly aware of Wenders, who having followed Amanda down the stairs, was now hovering in concern beside his master's elbow.

'I have laid out your riding clothes, Sir Robert,' he murmured. 'And Henderson has been told to bring you your musket and sword.'

'Yes, of course.' Sir Robert gave himself a mental shake and rose to his feet. 'And get as many of the staff who can use arms to mount and be prepared to leave, as soon as I give the word.'

To the untrained eye the next half hour represented turmoil, as servants rushed hither and thither to carry out their master's commands; but by the time Demonds returned, all of Sir Robert's staff capable of carrying arms were mounted, together with a contingent of Royalists summoned by Amanda.

But Sir Robert's biggest surprise was when George and Madeleine Randall trotted up, both dressed in men's clothes.

'She would come,' Lord Randall muttered. 'And she might be of some help. She's very handy with a pistol.'

'Whether or not she is, do you think you ought to be coming?' Sir Robert asked dubiously. 'You still look very unsteady.'

'They've got my boy,' Lord Randall said grimly. 'Nothing would keep me away. Now have our local colleagues been informed?'

'Yes, and there will be more,' Amanda explained. 'As we progress, men will join us from other parts of London and the outskirts. By the time we have a full complement, there should be about fifty of us.'

'Really.' Sir Robert tried to appear nonchalant, while still thinking of his small relatives. 'And can all these men be relied upon?'

'Absolutely,' Amanda and Lord Randall replied simultaneously.

It was not until they were galloping towards the village of Chelsea, that Sir Robert glanced back and was astonished to see how their number seem to have trebled since leaving Grosvenor Square. The increases continued until some hours later when they reached Woking where, Amanda explained, they would have to change their exhausted horses and rest for a few hours, so that everyone would be fully refreshed for any eventuality.

The ostler at *The Swan* did not appear at all surprised to see such a large number of armed men, nor did he comment on the equally-well armed women of the party. In fact, he was so unimpressed Sir Robert suspected he had been selected because he was a Royalist, and also knew how to keep his own counsel.

Despite the Randalls' obvious agitation, and Sir Robert's oft voiced concern regarding the children, Amanda insisted on waiting for the return of the three scouts sent out earlier to try and investigate what was happening at Hawton.

'We must know as much as possible, in order to prepare a successful attack,' she explained. 'It is most important that we are aware of the children's location, and just how much danger they are in. I know this sounds quite dreadful,' she added hurriedly in response to Lady Randall's startled expression. 'But it would be foolhardy to just rush in not knowing the whereabouts of the children beforehand. Ah, the scouts are back.'

This last remark was directed at the three men, one of whom was Demonds, who trotted into the Inn yard. Almost before the horse had stopped Demonds had sprung from the saddle and rushed over to Amanda.

'It's just as we thought,' he declared. 'There are only about thirty of them, and so far as we can gather no one in the area is aware of what has happened. The villagers appear to think the family have all returned to London, and taken most of their staff and the children with them. We have no idea how this tale has been spread unless, of course, you have a disloyal servant in your house?' he added, looking at Sir Robert.

'Impossible,' he replied heatedly. 'I'd vouch for every one of them. They've all been with my family for years. You know them,' he declared to Amanda. 'Don't you consider they're all loyal?'

She frowned. 'Of course, but don't you remember Mrs Honniton saying on her return to Hawton, that she had hired a sewing girl called Bridget Edgeley? Unfortunately, although her sewing was excellent, she has proved somewhat flighty and Mrs. Honniton told me only a few days ago that soon after joining Hawton, she had become friendly with one of the Kay's stable lads?'

'Are you sure?'

'Oh yes, she used to see him regularly in the village.'

'Merciful heaven, what has she done?'

'We don't yet know that she's done anything,' Amanda replied reassuringly. 'It is just that she is the only member of your staff with an outside friend. It could have been a perfectly harmless mistake on her part. She might have been asked when you were leaving, or even if you had left, and in all innocence answered the question. But it's no good speculating,' she added. 'What we have to do now is plan how we are going to invade the house. But first, Demonds, were you able to find out anything about the children?'

'Nothing at all, I'm afraid,' he replied. 'In fact the place looked deserted. Not a sign of life anywhere, and all the windows were covered with blinds. And the strangest thing,' he added, 'The church was closed as well.'

Sir Robert frowned. 'But that's not possible, the vicar and his family live very nearby and always ensure that the church door is kept ajar.'

'That's another thing,' Demonds said. 'The Manse looks uninhabited as well, with all the window blinds down. I think we need Sir Robert to draw us a plan of the house and out buildings, so that we can decide how to try and invade without being seen.'

Sir Robert immediately called for paper and ink, and under the guidance of a man called Scotton who explained he was an architect, drew a rough map of Hawton House and its outbuildings. After explaining to his guide the approximate width of the walls and entrance doors, Sir Robert shook his head.

'If there is nothing to be seen from the road, I can't imagine where they are hiding everyone.'

'But from your drawing,' Scotton said, 'the majority of windows appear to be at the front, and on the right hand side. What about the left side and the back of the house, where are their windows?'

'When the house was built, the owner only wanted the windows to face the sun. So there are no windows to the left of the house, and only the kitchen window at the back and that is shielded by the scullery area door.'

'Perfect,' Demonds said. 'So gentlemen, that's the way we will approach. The other thing is how loyal are your villagers?'

'I've no reason to believe they would betray me,' Sir Robert replied. 'But after all I've learned recently, I wouldn't like to be positive about anything.'

'Come, come, sir,' Rivers Newsome declared. 'The villagers would lay down their lives for you, and I'm sure if they knew there was anything wrong, they'd follow you immediately.'

Sir Robert flushed. 'Well ... thank you, Newsome, perhaps we should try and let them know what has happened.'

'No,' Barton, another of the riders said emphatically. 'That could cause chaos and innocent people could get hurt. Also, we have to remember that children are involved.'

At the mention of the children, everyone agreed that Demonds' strategy should be applied, and that if possible the people in the house should be overcome without anyone having to use their arms.

As it would take the rescuers at least another hour to reach the outskirts of the village, it was decided to dismount about half a mile from Hawton. Then, after splitting up into five groups, for four groups to approach the house with the fifth group bringing up the rear as reserve.

To Sir Robert, that half mile seemed endless and all he could think of were the two tiny scraps of humanity that had been placed in his arms so very long ago.

18

Over an hour later, moving very slowly through the undergrowth with Amanda a few feet ahead, Sir Robert was hardly aware that he was surrounded on all sides by other, fully armed men, so quiet were their movements as they progressed towards the house.

Suddenly there was the call of an owl, and in accordance with instructions Sir Robert sank to the ground and waited. Another call was then heard, and Barton appeared carrying a body which he laid gently down on the ground beside Sir Robert.

'I found him lying beside a tree further on. Do you know him?' Barton whispered.

Sir Robert stared down in consternation, because the figure lying at his feet covered in mud and with blood oozing from a cut on his head, was Nicholas Carter, the vicar's son.

'He's badly hurt,' Barton murmured. 'But if we could get him to recover a little, he might be able to tell us what's going on in the house.'

'I don't think he's going to be well enough,' Amanda said softly. 'But what's that?' she added staring into the undergrowth.

Immediately, Barton and his companion drew their swords, and Sir Robert was about to draw his pistol when a small figure seemed suddenly to fall out of the bushes.

'Great heaven,' Sir Robert exclaimed. 'It's Jack Fullerton, the lad I told you about,' he added to Lord Randall.

'Oh please, sir,' Jack began to gabble as soon as he recognised Sir Robert. 'Terrible things are happening in the house. They've taken everyone prisoner, even the vicar. Nicholas and me managed to get out, but Mick Taylor hit him on the head with a sword instead of me and ...'

'Mick Taylor!' Sir Robert declared, while Amanda shook her head warningly.

'Hush, hush, or we will be heard. Now child, you're quite safe so tell us what happened.'

'The men came during the night. There were a lot of them and they had guns and things, and they made all the servants go down into the wine cellar, but we others were put in different rooms.'

'Edward and Lucy ...?' Sir Robert began anxiously.

'We've hidden them in the ballroom with Hetty and Edgar, and the other three. You see, we were all on the upper landing when the men came, so we got them to be very quiet and we all crept into the minstrels' gallery in the ballroom, and then we told them to lie down and be quiet while we went for help. Then Nicholas took me into your library, Sir Robert, and we escaped through the secret passage, but Mick Taylor found us when we got out and that's when he hit Nicholas.'

'Secret passage, what secret passage?' Sir Robert asked, in surprise. 'There's never been a secret passage at Hawton.'

'Yes sir, it runs from the book room to the Manse and that's where Mick Taylor is, at the Manse.'

'But ...' Sir Robert began, only to be interrupted by Amanda.

'Never mind that now, have you any idea how many people there are in the Manse, Jack? And what happened with Mick Taylor; did he chase you?'

'I think he wanted to, but he was guarding the Manse servants; but he did say he'd skin me alive,' Jack added, looking very frightened.

'I don't think you need worry about that,' Sir Robert said, grimly. 'He's not going to have the chance of doing anything at all after we get him; and we can't leave Nicholas here. Shall we take him with us?'

'No, I suggest we leave him with Madeleine Randall, and two men to guard them,' Amanda said. 'Then, when all the insurgents have been arrested, they can join us.'

Having ascertained where everyone was imprisoned and how many guards were scattered about the Manse, Demonds, Amanda, and four other principal members of the group planned their invasion of Hawton, via the secret passage from the Manse.

As surprise was essential, it was agreed to attack before dawn and messengers were sent to the other three groups, telling them to await the signal, which would be two owl hoots.

As Sir Robert was determined to confront Mick Taylor, he joined Barton's group, which after freeing the Manse servants and imprisoning any of the marauders still there, would proceed up to the house to join the invasion of the building.

Having separated from the others Sir Robert's group approached the Manse expecting some sort of resistance, but to their surprise the building appeared deserted; and when they entered the only people they found were the eight Manse servants locked in the cellar; one of whom introduced herself as Mrs. Carter's personal maid.

'It was quite dreadful,' she declared nervously. 'They came at night and took the vicar and Mrs Carter, and they had weapons. The vicar tried to protect Mrs. Carter but he was overwhelmed, poor gentleman, and they tied him up with rope before dragging him away.'

'Just in case they come back,' Barton said. 'I suggest you all follow my friend here, and join some of our party still in the woods. You will be safe with them, since it appears all the intruders are now in the house. Now, young Jack, just where is this secret passage?'

Still very dubious as to the existence of this mystery, Sir Robert followed Jack into the Vicar's study, then watched in astonishment as the boy turned a knob of wood to the left of the fireplace, and very slowly, what appeared to be a door, swung open to reveal a flight of stone steps leading downwards.

'What on earth ...?' Sir Robert began but no one was listening because, in single file with Barton in the lead carrying a lighted candle, the rest of the party had commenced descending.

Following close behind, Sir Robert soon found himself in a narrow tunnel lined with walls exuding a heavy smell of damp. When at last Barton gave the signal to stop, Sir Robert realised that they must have reached his library wall and he strained his ears for any sound of life.

But all seemed eerily quiet, and he waited for Barton to give some signal as to their next move. Then surprisingly clear, considering the group's incarceration, Sir Robert heard the two hoots of an owl and Barton immediately thrust open the secret door to the library and sprang inside.

For a few moments there was pandemonium, as the occupants of the library tried to reach for their weapons, but Barton's men were too quick for them and the interlopers were soon huddled into a corner, and being guarded with three threatening guns.

Following his companions Sir Robert, intent on finding Edward and Lucy, made for the library door, but Barton shook head.

'No, wait, we have to be sure who is in the hall first and ... ah, I can hear that all our friends have arrived. Come on, men, into the hall!'

What followed afterwards Sir Robert always considered the most chaotic situation in which he had ever been involved. How on earth friend and foe were able to distinguish each other, he had no idea. All he could discern was the fact that one group appeared to be overcoming the other rapidly enough for the erstwhile intruders to be herded back into the library, to join the other prisoners still cowering against a far wall.

Out in the hallway, Barton now despatched groups to search different parts of the house, but as Sir Robert's only interest was the children, he ignored Barton, and followed by Jack ran up the stairs towards the ballroom.

On reaching the door he hesitated but unable to discern any sounds from within he entered, his revolver ready cocked. For a few seconds there was silence, then a medley of young voices began to yell down from the Minstrels' Gallery.

'We're up here.'

'We're ever so hungry.'

'We haven't made a noise.'

'Have the naughty men gone?'

Looking up Sir Robert sighed with relief to see Edgar, Edward, Lucy, the three other children and Hetty, all peering down over the edge of the gallery rail.

'Nicholas and Jack brought us up here. They were ever so brave,' Edgar called down. 'Now it's ...'

But before he could finish Lucy screamed: 'Uncle, look out!'

Sir Robert swung round in time to see a tall, heavily built man carrying a bull whip, reach out and grab Jack before holding him like a shield against his body.

'Thought you'd never see me again did you, you little guttersnipe. Skin you alive I said and skin you alive I will and then ...'

'So you're Mick Taylor,' Sir Robert said, drawing his sword. 'You were the man who sold this child for a pittance, and left his mother's body unshriven. Well man, let's see how you deal with someone your own size. On guard!'

Still holding Jack as protection Taylor threw back his whip, but before he could bring it back to hit Sir Robert Jack began to wriggle. Swearing, Taylor cuffed him hard and then threw him to the ground.

The brief lull was all Sir Robert needed, and with a leap he sprang forward and thrust his sword into Taylor's thigh. Cursing, the man fell to the ground still holding his whip, but Sir Robert wrenched it from his hands and gave him two cutting swipes on the small of his back.

To the accompaniment of loud clapping from all the other children, Sir Robert raised Jack gently to his feet.

'There, lad, I think you and your mother have been fully revenged,' he murmured. 'Master Taylor won't be selling any more young boys to chimney sweeps. In fact, I don't think he will be doing anything ever again after the law has dealt with him. Now, all of you up there, I suggest you come down and join us.'

With a considerable amount of noise and clatter the six children and Hetty descended down the wooden steps from the gallery, and Edward and Lucy flung themselves into their uncle's arms.

'We thought they were going to kill us,' Lucy declared indignantly. 'They were horrid, but Jack and Nicholas saved us.'

'Yes, Sir Robert,' Edgar said. 'They were very brave. They led us up there, and told us to be very quiet while they went for help.'

'What's all that noise?' Edward asked. 'Are the bad people being killed now, Uncle?'

'No, just being made prisoners, at least I think so,' Sir Robert added. 'So we must ...'

'So here you are! I wondered how long it would be before that bitch got you involved.'

Thrusting the children behind him, Sir Robert swung around to discover Lord Merton standing in the doorway, gripping his foil in one hand and a pistol in the other.

'Where is she, where is the bitch?' He snarled. 'If it wasn't for her meddling, we would have been able ...'

'For God's sake, David, you must be insane. How could you possibly think you could overthrow the monarchy?'

'Monarchy! You call a witless idiot and his batch of low life scum a monarchy? You're like all the rest, Robert, blinded by tradition and loyalty; and it's those sentiments that are turning this country into a wasteland which any other country could easily overpower. The Hanoverians are finished, and you're either with us or against us.'

Before Sir Robert could reply, the cries and sounds of fighting elsewhere in the house intensified and Lord Merton gave a coarse laugh.

'So, decide now, Robert. Join us or fight, and there'll be no quarter given, I swear.'

Sir Robert lowered his foil. 'I'll not fight you, David. So do your worst, but first let the children go.'

'You're a fool, Robert,' Lord Merton snarled, advancing. 'A fool and ...'

Simultaneously, Amanda sprang through the open doorway and the children ran screaming towards her. Gesturing to them that they should get behind her, she advanced towards Lord Merton with her épée extended.

'So you would draw on a friend, would you, sir? Well, I'm no friend so fight me first.'

Before Sir Robert could intervene, she had leapt at Lord Merton and their swords were slashing at each other with venom. Aghast, Sir Robert could only watch helplessly as the two assailants battled their way around the room. Then to his horror Amanda slipped, but before Lord Merton could thrust his foil into her side Sir Robert sprang at him and struck at his sword arm.

Bleeding heavily, Lord Merton swung round to defend himself, but an injured right-handed swordsman has no chance against a fit opponent, and Sir Robert had no difficulty in over-powering his assailant who fell heavily to the ground. Overcome with remorse at having injured his erstwhile friend Sir Robert had forgotten his previous assailant, and was too absorbed in assisting Lord Merton to realise that Mick Taylor had recovered enough to attack.

Amanda's cry: 'Robert, look out!' came too late for Sir Robert to defend himself against the piece of wood which Taylor aimed at his head; his last conscious sight was that of Amanda lunging at Taylor with her épée.

19

On regaining consciousness, Sir Robert discovered he was still in the ballroom, lying on a chaise longue with his very painful head in Lucy's lap.

'He's woken up,' she announced loudly.

'Thank goodness.' Amanda's voice seemed to echo in Sir Robert's ears. 'We were getting worried; that was a very large piece of wood.'

Sir Robert tried to raise himself only to be pushed gently back.

'You mustn't,' Lucy announced importantly. 'The doctor said you had to rest.'

'I'm perfectly all right,' Sir Robert insisted. 'And anyway, what's happened? Is everything over?'

'Yes, thank goodness,' Amanda replied, sitting on the edge of the chaise longue. 'There was never really any doubt that they would not succeed. Mainly because a great number of their so-called followers had voiced their loyalty, but as we suspected, when they realised the enormity of what they were about to attempt, it subdued their enthusiasm. But we were still worried about the publicity they would have attracted, had they been able to hold

Hawton against us. There has to be change in England but anarchy is definitely not the answer.'

'Where is everyone, and what have you done with Merton? And what of Alice and the children, what will she do?'

'As a traitor he's liable for the death sentence,' Amanda explained. 'But I rather think he will be given the alternative of permanent exile as a convict, which will mean deportation to the Australias. That way he will just be one of many, whereas anything more drastic would gain a great deal of publicity which, as I said before, we do not want. As for Alice ...' Amanda sighed. 'She knows nothing at all about this, and it is going to be an enormous shock, but she does have her parents and family to support her and she will, of course, still have all Merton's lands and wealth.'

'Where is he?'

'Downstairs in your library, with the other four leaders of the group. All the other prisoners are shackled and being guarded by your staff in the cellar As for our friends, most have left to return to London, but there are fifteen or so still here waiting to escort the prisoners back to the city tomorrow for trial. But why do you ask about Merton? You surely don't want to see him?' Amanda said, looking askance.

Sir Robert struggled to his feet, much to Lucy's annoyance.

'The doctor said ...' she began.

'Yes, sweetheart, I know,' Sir Robert replied gently, 'but I really am all right now, and I have to do something.'

Considering his house had only two or three hours earlier been used as a battleground, Sir Robert was surprised at the orderliness of all the interior, and the fact that on encountering Mrs. Honniton in the corridor, the good lady merely smiled and continued on her way as if nothing had happened.

Reaching the library door, Sir Robert found the entrance guarded by Charles Henderson and Archer.

'I want to see Lord Merton,' Sir Robert said. 'Mrs. Brace told that me he's in here.'

'Yes, Sir Robert,' Henderson said. 'He's with the French gentleman, and his friends. They're being closely guarded by some of the gentlemen from London. But Lord Merton's quite poorly, I'm afraid. The doctor's given him something for the pain and to help him sleep. So I don't know how he is at the moment.'

'Really,' Sir Robert said with a brief nod. 'So long as he's in there, that's all I need to know.'

But on entering Sir Robert realised that David Merton, lying stretched out on a chaise longue, was indeed barely conscious, and also seemed unaware of either his surroundings or the fact that he was being closely guarded by men Sir Robert recognised as having been part of Barton's invading party.

They were all armed, but from the dejected appearance of the other four prisoners there was little doubt that they would cause any trouble. Kay, the only one Sir Robert recognised, looked exhausted, as did two of his three companions, all of whom wore manacles on their ankles and wrists. The only individual without chains was a thin pale bespectacled man of indiscriminate age, almost crouching in his chair. For some reason he reminded Sir Robert of someone, but being intent on speaking to Lord Merton, he dismissed the thought from his mind.

Despite their violent encounter in the ballroom, Sir Robert was pleased to see that his erstwhile friend was not wearing any form of restraint, and preferring to speak to Lord Merton in private he indicated to the armed guards that they should leave the room and wait outside the door. Ignoring their obvious reluctance, Sir Robert waited until the door closed then, unsure whether or not Lord Merton was still unconscious, softly murmured his name; whereupon the prisoner slowly opened his eyes.

'Come to gloat, have you?' he muttered.

'Of course not, don't be ridiculous,' Sir Robert said sharply. 'I've come to see if I can help regarding Alice and the children.'

'Ah, Robert Masters, the ever-lasting philanthropist. What do they say, "Spread your ... something ... on the water so that it can return to you" ?'

'Something like that,' Sir Robert replied. 'Why did you kill that poor girl?'

'Had to, old chap, she was in the pay of that termagant you intend to make your wife. Our plans were too important to be scuppered by a mere wench. And by the way, allow me to introduce you to our hero of the hour, the rightful king, if ever there was one ...'

Lord Merton raised himself slightly and bowed in the direction of the pale man, who was now asleep and snoring softly. Sir Robert stared at him, and then realised with something of a shock that although there was only a vague likeness, it was as if the arrogant features of long dead Charles Stuart, the Bonnie Prince Charlie of historical fame, were now glancing up at him.

Sir Robert shook his head in disbelief. 'Incredible, did he really want to usurp the king? Did he realise what you were all making him do?'

Lord Merton sank back onto his pillow. 'He seemed to, but after we took this place he seemed to lose interest. In fact, he seemed to think he was just attending a country gathering until Kay explained everything to him.'

'So he didn't know what his destiny was going to be?' Sir Robert remarked, dryly.

'I don't think so. Now, what's this about Alice?'

'Before we discuss your family, there is one other matter I would like to mention,' Sir Robert said lowering his voice. 'Does the name Dorothy Lesley bring back any memories?'

Lord Merton frowned. 'Should it?'

'I think so, since the son she gave birth to, after assisting in your recovery from a riding accident some eight year ago, is now living in this house under my protection.'

Lord Merton stared uncomprehendingly at Sir Robert. 'Eight years ago, for pity's sake, Robert.'

'You don't remember a village in Wiltshire, a kind doctor who took you in and his daughter who nursed you? Or did you, and do you still deflower kind women after they have administered to your welfare?'

Lord Merton's expression darkened and he flushed heavily. 'By God, Robert, if I was not a ...'

'You truly do not remember her, not at all?'

'I've had enough of this.' Lord Merton's response was more of a snarl than a reply. 'If you insist, I remember only that I lost a valuable mare from that deuced accident, and was forced to remain supine for three days while some wench assisted the doctor administering to me.'

Sir Robert's disgust was so evident in his expression, Lord Merton stared at him in obvious perplexity.

'S'truth, Robert, surely you don't expect me to remember every dalliance, do you, and if that one ...'

'That particular dalliance, as you describe it,' Sir Robert replied, struggling to control his revulsion, 'resulted in a son, for whom you will make an annual recompense if you wish Alice to remain ignorant of his existence. And as, so I have been told, your future life will be one of travail in a foreign country far from these shores, I think it wise for all your financial responsibilities to be concluded while you remain in this house. I will arrange for Sinclair to draw up the necessary documents immediately.'

Without waiting for Merton's response, Sir Robert turned and left the room. Once outside he leaned against the door breathing heavily, and his three retainers stared at him in concern.

'Are you all right, Sir Robert?' Newsome asked anxiously. 'You're as pale as a sheet.'

'It's nothing, nothing,' Sir Robert muttered. 'But I must find Sinclair; do you know where he is?'

Having explained to his steward what was required, Sir Robert climbed wearily to the children's rooms where Amanda was supervising their evening meal.

'My dear,' she declared, as Sir Robert entered. 'You look exhausted, perhaps you ought to rest.'

'I've been with Merton,' he muttered, lowering himself onto the nearest chair. 'The man is a ...'

'Now, children,' Amanda interrupted quickly. 'Would you like to return to the ballroom, and play bat and ball before bedtime?'

There was a unanimous cry of 'Yes', and within seconds, Sir Robert and Amanda were alone.

'Now, my dearest of men, tell me what has happened,' Amanda murmured, snuggling down on Sir Robert's knee.

He shook his head. 'The man's a blackguard; he's not only a murderer, he's a seducer as well.' With a deep sigh, Sir Robert told her all that had passed between himself and Lord Merton.

'Poor, poor, Alice,' Amanda said. 'But Lizzie Cooper is a good friend, as well as a loving sister so hopefully she will be able to give support. But what a detestable man. I was correct; he will be deported, probably as soon as possible to avoid publicity. I gather from Godfrey, that's Demonds' real name,' she added with a laugh, 'that arrangements are being made for him to be taken secretly to Portsmouth, in order that he can leave on the first available boat.'

'So we must let Alice know what has happened as soon as possible,' Sir Robert said with a deep sigh. 'What an appalling, stupid, mess.'

Some time later, having gained Lord Merton's signature to a financial settlement on Jack, and the remainder of his fortune and all his estates to be handed over to Alice Merton in trust for their eldest son, Sir Robert joined Amanda for dinner in the library.

'What about the prisoners' escort for tomorrow, is everyone else being fed?' he asked, as he poured her some wine.

'Oh, goodness, yes,' she said with a laugh. 'After the children went to bed, Mrs Honniton arranged for tables to be erected in the ballroom, and everyone who isn't a prisoner is in there. The prisoners ate their meal earlier, and it was probably the last good one they will ever have. Such foolish folk, especially the Kays, who will lose everything for their treachery.'

'What's happened to the erstwhile king?'

'Oh, he was taken away after you saw David Merton. Godfrey arranged for a carriage to take him to Dover, and he is being escorted back to Paris. I am convinced he is still ignorant of his real role in all this. As is,' she added, dropping her voice, 'our established monarch, or his successor.'

'It has all been an appalling fiasco,' Sir Robert declared. 'Except, that if it had not happened, we might never have met and that would have been a tragedy. Now,' he leaned forward and took up her left hand gently in his own, 'we have more serious matters to discuss, our marriage for instance.'

20

In accordance with their wishes, the wedding was a quiet affair at St. George's in Hanover Square, with few guests and little ceremony. Elevated to a position of prominence, Wenders officiated with aplomb by giving the bride away, while all the children insisted on supporting the bride; so Lucy was a flower girl, while all the boys were pages, escorting the bride up the aisle.

The few guests that attended were mainly staff from both London and Hawton, with only a very few of Sir Robert's and Amanda's closest friends. Too many people had been harmed during the past events for too much jollity, and their painful and tragic interview with Alice Merton had proved almost too distressing for Sir Robert and Amanda to bear.

At first, the poor woman had refused to believe them, declaring that Sir Robert had always been jealous of her husband and now wanted to humiliate him. But when Amanda insisted on asking her as to where Lord Merton was at that precise moment, she broke down and admitted that he had left the house a week earlier and she had not seen him since.

Gently but firmly she was given the humiliating truth that her husband was a condemned traitor, who had already been deported to Australia and that as a result she would probably never see him again.

She was spared the revelations that he was both a murderer and seducer, as these crimes were not included in those levelled against him. After Sir Robert's attempts at persuasion, the judiciary agreed, that as there were five children to consider who, like their mother, were entirely ignorant of Lord Merton's infamy, having a father for a traitor was going to be hard enough for them to bear. To have included his other appalling misdemeanours might have had dire consequences on the children's future as adults.

This distressing interview was the reverse of the one Madeleine Randall insisted on having, with Jack's grandfather.

Determined to discover whether Doctor Lesley was still alive, she had insisted on sending a servant to the doctor's village to seek him out. After an anxious five days, the man returned with the happy news that Doctor Lesley was alive and still residing in the same house he had once shared with his daughter.

'He must be told he has a grandson,' Lady Randall insisted. 'And surely it is only fair to let Jack know he is not completely alone in the world.'

'But what if Mr. Lesley wants to keep Jack,' Amanda asked. 'Edgar would be so upset at losing his friend.'

'We will have to risk that eventuality,' Lady Randall insisted. 'To deny them both the chance of knowing each other exists would be wrong.'

So it was, that on one spring day in April, Doctor Lesley was surprised to see a very handsome carriage with a crest pull up at his garden gate. Believing that the travellers were seeking directions to a place elsewhere he hurried out; but the man and woman who descended, instead of enquiring directions, requested a moment of his time in private.

Somewhat perplexed, since it was obvious they were titled folk, Doctor Lesley escorted them into his house and offered them some refreshment.

'Thank you, sir,' Lady Randall said gently. 'But we just wished to have a few minutes of your time to explain who we are, and why we are here.'

The resultant revelation reduced the good doctor to tears, as he explained that, after she left his house he had never heard from his daughter again.

'I thought she had possibly eloped with some unsuitable man,' he explained shakily, 'and when I heard nothing, I assumed that possibly she was dead. I never for one moment imagined she might have been enciente, and it was a son. Why, oh why, didn't she tell me?'

Slowly and very gently they explained how Jack had been educated by his mother, his appalling fate at the hands of Mick Taylor, and his eventual rescue by Sir Robert.

'He formed a close friendship with our own son, Edgar,' Lady Randall explained. 'And before knowing his history, we agreed to adopt him and raise him as our own. But now, in view of the fact that he is not without family, we thought it only right that you should be aware of his existence.'

'Indeed, indeed, and thank you for coming, I am most grateful.' Doctor Lesley shook his head. 'Nearly eight years old you say. Well, well. I should indeed like to see him, and become acquainted, but I am now elderly and do not practise any more. You say he has formed a friendship with your son. Well, perhaps they would both like to visit me. I think it would be easier for him, Jack, you say; ah, that is my name. She called him Jack, Why, oh why didn't she tell me, my poor Dorothy. How her mother would have grieved to hear all this. Oh dear, I feel quite moved.'

Although the meeting proved so emotional, it ended on an optimistic and delightful note; arrangements were made for Jack to visit Doctor Lesley in company with Edgar, and for him to remain under the care of the Randalls, with regular holiday visits to his grandfather.

Because Sir Robert had been the initial instigator of Jack's freedom, he received this wonderful news from him, and to Sir Robert's relief, was ecstatic rather than emotionally moved.

'A grandfather, oh Sir Robert, I belong to someone after all,' he declared excitedly. 'When can I meet him? What's he like? Will he like me? What about Edgar?'

When everything had been explained to his satisfaction, Jack rushed away to tell Edgar the wonderful news.

And of course he insisted that his three erstwhile companions should share his joy, which resulted in Matthew, Mark, and Timothy not only inheriting a *relative,* but also acquiring an intense interest in Doctor Lesley's profession, which eventually led them to successful careers in different branches of medicine.

So regardless of the plots and their consequences, life for all concerned returned to as normal a state as was possible. Napoleon remained on St. Helena, dreaming of rescue and resurrection while basking in the Balcombes' adoration; Lady Merton, having been assured that the reappearance of her husband was most unlikely, eventually remarried and changed the family name to Waterson; while Jack and Edgar continued to revel in having two homes and a shared grandfather.

And despite the low opinion in which the Prince Regent was held, he did succeed to the throne of England without any further disturbances and reigned for ten years, blissfully unaware of any attempts to dislodge him!

As for Wenders, despite being elevated to the position of brother-in-law to nobility, he was convinced that no one else could perform his tasks better than he did and refused to relinquish his position as valet.

Perhaps the only two people not altogether satisfied with their lot were the erstwhile usurper and David Merton. The former, because he never did quite understand what had happened, and remained convinced he had been cheated out of a country estate rather than a kingdom; and the latter because although he managed to persuade the authorities to let him eke out his sentence working as a stable hand, rather than as a stone breaker, he could not resist attempting to seduce his master's daughter. This act of depravity resulted in her outraged father, an individual of some standing, having Merton despatched to an area of Western Australia where he was forced to spend his remaining days amongst the worst criminals ever sentenced for deportation.

The happiness and contentment that Sir Robert and his adored Amanda found in each other was intensified with the birth of twin daughters, much to the delight of Edward and Lucy. This joy was repeated two years later, when twin brothers joined the family, bringing the total number of children within Hawton's sheltering walls to nine.

It was while discussing what the future might hold for the children, especially their adopted sons whose lives would have been so very different but for their chance meeting with Sir Robert, that the Masters made the momentous decision to turn Hawton into a home for deprived orphans.

'After all,' Sir Robert murmured to a friend, 'there are so many children who need help, and with all the babies and children already here, I don't think the staff will really notice another twelve or so!'